HAPPILY EVER AFTER

The reason teenagers are so screwed up is that all the stuff people tell you when you're a kid you find out is lies when you're a teenager. Maybe they should have told us there's no enchanted place and some people are just plain ugly and ever after doesn't last that long . . .

novels by

RACHEL VAIL:

WONDER

DO-OVER

EVER AFTER

DARING TO BE ABIGAIL

NEVER MIND!

IF WE KISS

THE FRIENDSHIP RING:

If You Only Knew

Please, Please, Please

Not That I Care

What Are Friends For?

Popularity Contest

Fill In the Blank

one

SOMETHING'S MISSING. I just spent five minutes staring into the refrigerator, but it wasn't in there. Too bad what's missing isn't no-fat mayonnaise. I think I need a secret place nobody knows about except me and maybe one special friend—a boy, probably—and we would say cute but profound things to each other there. In the movies, kids always have an enchanted spot they go to when they're sad—usually a willow tree or down by the railroad tracks. Maybe that's what I'm missing.

Or maybe the whole enchanted spot thing is a creation of frustrated screenwriters who never had one when they were growing up, either. Maybe they felt all the time like something was missing, too, and since they couldn't find it in the refrigerator, they made up the enchanted spot cliche. Maybe it's a cruel joke or initiation like the whole Santa Claus business, invented so you'll know when you've stopped being a kid: after you face the emotional devastation of figuring out that your most cherished part of life was a fake. You're less and less a kid, by degrees, depending on how few of the lies you buy. I'd say, if that's true, I'm about between 70 and 80 percent no longer a kid, because there's not that much I believe in anymore, but I still have no urge to try to get younger kids to buy any bull, either, which I gotta figure, along with being able to read a thermometer, means you're an adult.

I keep picturing myself being twenty-five, talking to my fiance or whatever and laughing about what I was like this summer before high school. Then he'll call the waiter over for the check and help me on with my coat, and we'll say how we wish we could be kids again because it was all so sweet. Oh, please.

So I'm going to write down the truth of how it is right now, while it's still now, in this blank book that my best friend Vicky bought me for my birthday. Vicky said she thought of me as soon as she saw it.

"Why?" I asked her, hugging the book to show her how much I liked it. The cover is burgundy marbled with gray, and it's the classiest-looking thing I ever got.

"It just seemed like something you would like. Feel the paper."

I opened it. The paper was thick and textured. "Nice," I said.

"I got it in June," she said, "when my mother and I took the ferry off-island to get my summer clothes in Boston. And I got into that whole thing with her—remember I told you?"

I nodded. Vicky gets into a whole thing with her mother every time they try to do anything together.

"I was like, Get me out of here, so I went up to the front of the store and they had all these books. I opened one up and felt the paper and thought of you. I don't know why. I guess I was wishing you had come with us." She smiled at me, then touched the cover of the book. "And then when they had this one with the burgundy and gray . . ."

"My favorite colors."

"I know. Because your mother likes red and black."

"That's not why. I just like burgundy and gray. I always have."

"Whatever," she said. She picked up the wrapping paper I had dropped on the living-room rug and stomped into the kitchen with it. Vicky is the best friend anyone could ever have. You have to be careful what you say, though. I guess that's true with anybody. Sometimes I'm very insensitive.

When she came back, I hugged my new journal again. "I love it," I said. "It's perfect."

She smiled slowly and then sat down again next to me on the couch. I smiled back. We've been best friends a long time. "Since there are no lines," she said, taking the journal from me, "you can write as big or small as you want, or doodle, or whatever."

"Excellent," I said.

I told her I'd write this pretending it's a letter to a pen pal and include all the details of what happens to me, but instead of sending it to some stranger in Japan or something like we had to do last year in school (neither of ours ever wrote back), I'll write it to the me of the future. Vicky thought that was a great idea.

Dear Future Me,

Hi. How are you? I'm fine. Sort of.

Before I forget, while I'm still only, say, 78 percent grown up, I'm going to write down what's going on, and hopefully that will stop you, Future Me, from cheapening it later. Maybe it will also help me slow it down enough to hold on to this last 22 percent for a while. How did I feel when I was seven? It's so hard to remember. I think mostly I felt happy. Anxious for my teeth to start falling out, because I was a little late for that. Everybody else had missing teeth and my baby teeth embarrassed me, but mostly I felt safe. Or maybe that's not how it was; maybe I just forgot. Here I am, wishing I could be seven again because it was so sweet and safe, when maybe being seven was stressed-out, too.

I can't wait to grow up and get my period and my own phone and a waist, to stay up for "Letterman" and fall in love, but the thing is, what I wouldn't want to admit to anybody (especially Grace, my new friend) is I *like* being a kid. Sometimes I don't think I'm ready for all this stuff I've started doing and thinking about. Maybe I need to be left back as a thirteen-year-old. If I could just take a break, that would be really good.

But no, I'm fourteen today, my first totally unimportant birthday. I told Mom and Dad fourteen is too old to have such a fouffy room. They said okay, so for my birthday they're getting me a new platform bed from the Conran's catalog instead of this ridiculous canopy thing, and this morning Dad and his friend Walter painted over my incredibly prissy flowered wallpaper with solid navy blue semi-gloss.

I'm lying here on this old bed for one of the last times, feeling totally sick. When I was little, I used to play in here alone, pretending I was a princess and Mom and

Dad were queen and king and together we killed the dragon or whatever, and then I waited here on my bed under my canopy for the prince to come marry me. The part of the prince was usually played by the purple flower on my wallpaper, and sometimes I kissed it. Sometimes when I was little, I acted out the whole wedding of me and Prince Purple Flower. He was so madly in love with me, he gave up his kingdom to live here on Leeward Island with me and Mom and Dad. While I slept, he would watch me to make sure I was okay, and we all lived happily ever after.

Prince Purple Flower got painted over today while I was helping out at Mom's nail salon. I'm no longer a beautiful little princess; I'm a moderately unpopular pre-ninth-grade brace-faced bookworm with a zit on my chin, puffy hair, glasses, and bitten-down cuticles, mourning a painted-over prince who was really just a faded section of wallpaper.

The reason teenagers are so screwed up is because all the stuff people tell you when you're a kid you find out is lies when you're a teenager. All that enchanted place and you could be president and happily ever after and everybody's beautiful crap. Maybe they should've told us there's no such place and some people are just plain ugly and ever after doesn't last that long right from the beginning.

6

two

IT'S GOOD THAT there aren't dates on the pages of this book like in the diary I had when I was little, because it's still today and here I am, writing again already.

I'm stressed.

The ceiling is so far away, and I feel totally unsheltered under it. Not that a pink fouffy canopy could protect me or that my ceiling is something I need to be protected against, but I guess I was used to it. When we got home from dinner, Dad took apart my bed and brought it down to the basement in pieces. The new one is coming tomorrow, but for now I have only the mattress on the floor and the smell of new paint making me dizzy, like Mom warned it would. We had a discussion about it after we dropped off Grace and Vicky. Mom and Dad wanted me to sleep in the guest room, but they let me do what I wanted because it's still my birthday. I think they were so happy for me that I had more than just Vicky to invite out to dinner this year.

When Vicky and I were young, her brother, Henry, used to baby-sit for us. He told us there was a bad guy who slit open the throats of little kids who stayed up past their bedtimes. Pretty sick baby-sitter, terrifying and trau-matizing us so he could watch TV alone earlier. What a jerk he used to be. Now he's nineteen and not a jerk at all.

But anyway, I got used to sleeping with my fist curled against my neck to protect it from being slit, because I always stayed up past my bedtime reading with a flash-light, and I knew my days were numbered. That's what I said to myself as I was falling asleep: My days are num-bered. And then I'd ball my little fist under my chin, as if some bad guy with a machete breaking into the house and slipping into my room in the middle of the night to murder me for annoying Henry by staying up past nine or whatever would see my fist against my throat and have to leave to find an unprotected neck to slit. I got into the habit, though, and now I can't sleep without my hand rolled under my chin. And the same with my canopy. It's stupid but I can't sleep without it.

I should count backward like when you get put under anesthesia. If they really do that. Maybe they only do that in movies; I wouldn't know, never having been put under anesthesia myself. Why would they have you count backward? Does it make you go under faster? One hundred, ninety-nine, ninety-eight—I'm still up, staring at my ceiling. There's a crack in it that looks like nothing. Creative people like Grace are always seeing profound things in cracks and clouds. I just see cracks and clouds. Ninety-seven, ninety-six, ninety-five—this definitely isn't working. Maybe I'll count forward and back and meet in the middle and fall asleep between forty-nine and fifty. Right? Or fifty and fifty-one? One, one hundred; two, ninety-nine; three, ninety-eight—this is much too boring. My mind is already wandering, and I'm thinking about thinking and trying to figure out how many tracks I can think on at once. Like now I'm thinking about thinking, but as soon as I think that, it means I'm thinking about thinking about thinking, then thinking about thinking about. . . on and on and I can't count how many tracks, but now I am totally wide-awake and sitting up, very far below my ceiling.

Does everybody feel this weird? Like, is this adulthood? Do you get used to this? Or does this pass? Or is it just me who feels so weird?

It's 2:37, and I'm still awake and not at all psyched. I wish I could run away, only I have nowhere to go, no enchanted spot, no way off this island. I'm stuck here. I'm so stuck I don't know what to do. People like Grace who come to Leeward Island for the summer think it's an escape; how would they feel if they could never leave?

I wish I had a friend, a real friend with her own line, and I could just call her up and tell her I'm feeling so low, so sad and alone, and she would say, Hold on, I'll be right over. Just once if I could really connect with somebody and feel really okay being together. If I could just be totally myself and not tense with somebody, stop worrying for an hour does she like me, am I being weird or insensitive or unlikable. Sometimes when I'm talking, like with Grace or Vicky, I hear myself say something and I think, Who said that? I don't even agree with myself half the time. I'm so busy trying to be nice I forget to think. Sometimes I feel like I'm watching a movie about this girl named Molly, but it has very little to do with me.

I wish I could stop being so lonely. I keep looking over to where Prince Purple Flower used to be, and all I see is navy blue paint. I wanted this, I wanted the whole room, even the ceiling, painted dark blue to match my rug so I would feel like I was floating in the night sky. I thought that would be really cool, but it turns out I get nauseated, floating. And I keep looking at that space on my wall. It's weird—I didn't realize I still looked at Prince Purple Flower to fall asleep.

For a while last year, I pretended Prince Purple Flower was Jason Aronson, and I fell asleep thinking about if he'd smile when I got on the bus the next morning. Maybe I'll cry a little about Jason not liking me anymore, about maybe being too ugly and too slutty. I never should have made out with him behind the toolshed that time. Vicky said that's probably why he broke up with me. I don't think that's why—we just kissed, which I don't think is slutty, and obviously I wasn't the only one kissing, so if I'm a slut, he is, too—but I may be wrong. I wonder if he's noticed that I need to wear a bra now, and if he has noticed, if he likes it. I don't like it. I've been wearing really big sweatshirts for the past month, even though it was July. I feel like I'm taking up too much room lately.

Which means it's definitely too late for me to become an Olympic gymnast. That is totally depressing. Not that I failed in the Olympic trials or something; I can't even do a decent cartwheel. But it just hit me that for the first time in my life, I'm too old to make a particular career choice. And I'm not taking advanced math next year, which basically counts out being an engineer when I grow up, too. Doors are slamming in my face, and I'm killing time, watching the clock: 3:17. Not my birthday anymore, not July anymore, not the first half of summer anymore, not a kid anymore.

I thought being a teenager was supposed to be this big deal, the best time in my life. Great. I'm just growing out of all my clothes, and Daddy doesn't call me Minute anymore. He used to call me Molly Minute because he said I was only as big as a minute. Now I'm about an hour and a half. Oh, that's a catchy nickname—maybe Dad could call me Hour-and-a-half.

I asked Mom this morning over English muffins (with birthday candles stuck in the cottage cheese on top) what's special about me. I mean, Grace is a great soprano and wild, not to mention rich. She gave me a gold bracelet for my birthday. Vicky is an artist and also the most intense, extreme person I've ever met. But what am I? I'm fourteen already, and I have no idea who I am. Mom said, "You're a nice person." Thanks a lot, Mom. How fascinating that makes me sound. Nice. Terrific.

Is this my life? Every afternoon is filled up with lessons in stuff I don't give a crap about and stink in, to various degrees, like ballet and saxophone. I jog to The Nail Place every morning and have never been late, even though I am an embarrassingly slow runner and do nothing useful once I get there. I have only two friends; they both bug me. I'm afraid of my ceiling. I'm nice.

If I had somebody to like, I think it would be better, just somebody to think about when the radio is on or when I practice the saxophone, because practically every song is I love you, or I used to love you, or you used to love me, or something like that. The whole love thing doesn't sound like that great an idea, actually. But still, I need somebody to picture and think about and doodle my name with his. I wish I had a brother like Henry who would introduce me to his cool nineteen-year-old friends, and we could go driving up-island in a convertible with my guy's arm around me in the backseat. His name would be Winston and he wouldn't talk much, except to me, and we would feel so passionate about each other it would be hard to breathe. And my brother would call me Minute just like Dad used to.

It's starting to get light out.

three

I'VE BEGUN A life of crime. I may become a profes-
sional thief when I get older, because although I take lessons in everything my mother can find to sign me up for,
stealing (with one small exception) seems to be the only
thing I am naturally good at. Actually, crime may not be
a terrible career choice. Eventually I would hit rock
bottom and reform, and then I could get off-island and
travel around the country speaking to schoolchildren very
authentically, saying, Look, I've been there. An ex-druggie
came to our school last year; it was very powerful.

I don't know what I expected. Maybe bells going off
and Mr. Clark, the old guy who owns the drug-store, grabbing my arm and saying, "Ah-*ha*! Caught ya red-handed!"

Those were the exact words I expected, even heard in my head as I slipped the roll of Life Savers into my shorts pocket.

When we got outside, I grabbed Grace by the wrist and dragged her down the street. I was sweating and my heart was pumping so hard I was sure I was about to have a heart attack, and all I could think was, If I die of a heart attack right here on Centre Street, and the paramedics come, they will discover this roll of Passion Fruit Life Savers in my pocket and somehow the whole sordid tale will come out, and my parents will not just be in mourning but disgraced as well.

I didn't let go of Grace until we got down to the docks.

"What the hell?" She pushed her hair out of her eyes with her thumb and pinkie. I love how she does that and I'm starting to copy but her bangs are more grown out than mine, so it's more convincing on her. By the time school starts, though, maybe.

I took a deep breath and pulled the Passion Fruits Life Savers out of my pocket. I let them lie in my palm so she could look at them.

"What?"

I opened my eyes wide at her so she would understand.

"You what? You scungillied them?"

"I what?"

"That's what we call it at home," she explained. Grace lives in Manhattan during the year. They do everything early in Manhattan. Her sister, Simone, who is only eleven, has already French-kissed. She has a sister named Simone, of all things—leave it at that. And her sister *looks* like a Simone. If my name were Grace or Simone, I'd still look like a Molly.

"Oh," I said.

She picked up the roll and looked at it. "This isn't the first time you've ever scungillied, is it?"

"No," I lied. Sure, I do it all the time. That's why my teeth are sweating.

"I was gonna say . . ."

She took the roll and indented with her thumbnail in between the two middle Life Savers. Then she broke the pack in half and handed one section to me.

"I like Tropical Fruits better," she said, and walked down the dock toward the water. I looked at my half of the stolen Life Savers. May as well eat one, I thought, but when I put one in my mouth, it tasted terrible to me and I had to spit it out, right into the harbor. I hope a fish doesn't try to eat it and choke.

"Is that Vicky's brother's boat?"

I looked out to the sailboat Grace was pointing at. It was a Soling, which is what they have, but I couldn't really see it well enough to be positive. "Yeah, I think so," I said.

"Vicky's lucky," Grace said, unwrapping the Life Savers into her palm.

"I know it," I said. "You're both lucky. I mean, she has Henry, you have Simone. Who do I have? Nobody."

I stuck the half pack minus one back in my shorts pocket and sat down next to Grace. The one small exception to my planned life of crime is that I don't think I would ever be able to enjoy what I stole. Grace dumped her whole half pack into her mouth at once.

"No, I mean, he's hot," she said with her mouth full. She already has a lot of cavities. She says it's hereditary and all the brushing and apples in the world wouldn't make a difference; that's just hype put out by the American Dental Association.

"Yeah," I said. "He teaches me saxophone."

"I know," she said. "You always say that."

I laughed even though it wasn't funny, but that's what I do when I don't know what to say. The only reason someone as obviously cool as Grace would be friends with me is because she had nobody but her little sister to hang around with until she met me and Vicky in the arcade on the Fourth of July. As much as her sister does look like a Simone, an eleven-year-old is an eleven-year-old. Not to belittle myself, but honestly. "I'd be happy just even to have a little sister."

"I wonder what he kisses like," Grace said.

"He has a girlfriend from college."

"I never saw him with a girl."

"She's supposed to be getting here today. Her family is from South Carolina or South Dakota or something."

"So what? He always looks at you."

"He does not."

"I saw him," she said. "When he picked Vicky up from your house that day."

"I was standing on the porch, he was looking out the windshield."

"He looked at you, I swear."

"As if," I said. "You want these?" I held out my half of the Life Savers. "I don't even like Life Savers."

I should've been caught, is the thing. Kids on After School Specials would get caught. They would have to go back in and apologize and learn their lesson. How am I supposed to learn my lesson? Maybe now I'll go on to worse and worse things. Maybe I am one of those kids who were born without a conscience.

Fat chance. I'm a wreck over a roll of Life Savers. I'll probably never steal another thing. I feel guilty about everything. I think I only stole in the first place because I felt guilty about being too goody-goody. I need some vices. I don't drink or have sex or even listen to music very loud because the noise gives me a headache. All the statistics about how wild kids are today leave me out. Liking whole milk instead of skim is my one vice. Holey moley, put me on *America's Most Wanted*. If I weren't me, I almost definitely wouldn't choose me as a friend. I like people who have some danger in them, some tragedy in their souls, some spirit or excitement. Like Vicky. Like Grace. I think if I weren't me, I wouldn't like me because I'm too vanilla.

But I did commit a crime. That's something.

Oh, great, stealing a roll of Life Savers makes me a really fascinating person. A big sixty cents and I still feel so guilty I washed the dishes after dinner, trying in some cosmic way to atone. Some rebel. I'm doomed, totally doomed. Grace was completely underwhelmed, and there's no way I'm ever telling Vicky. She would be appalled, but not in a way like I was wild and dangerous, more like stupid and a jerk. I wish I had a little sister named Simone or maybe Marya. I would go into her room, and we would lie head to toe in her canopy bed and I would tell her I stole. She would say, Really? Were you scared? And we would sometimes sneak into each other's room after bedtime and tell each other our secrets, and she would idolize me. Even if I seemed like a boring person to the rest of the world, she would think I was amazing and follow me and my friends around the way Simone does with Grace. I might pretend to be annoyed but secretly I wouldn't be, because she'd be my lifelong best friend.

four

I'M TAKING ALL this throwing up as punishment.
Mom says it's a virus, but I didn't tell her about scungilli.

I couldn't write in here at all yesterday, even though I
had vowed to write every single day. Sorry, Future Me who
is reading this; I'll try to catch up. Actually there's nothing
to say about yesterday except I felt horrible, mostly
because I knew I deserved to. There, I'm caught up.

This afternoon I finally ate half a piece of toast without puking, so Mom said Vicky could stop by to visit. I
took a shower before she came. It totally wiped me out.

"You look good," Vicky said when she came into the
guest room. Once my birthday passed, Mom made me
move in here. She thinks if it's not a virus making me
puke, it was the fumes.

"As if," I said.

"No, I meant it," Vicky answered. She has a very deep, scratchy voice for a thirteen-year-old, especially someone so tiny. Like she has perpetual laryngitis, like she was up late last night talking about deep issues or at a rock concert. Our math teacher last year thought Vicky's voice was really sexy, which mortified Vicky and started me on this thing of trying to yell as abrasively as possible when I'm alone so I'll lose my voice, too.

"Thanks." I pushed back my bangs with my thumb and pinkie. Vicky looked away. She doesn't like Grace that much, I think. Maybe it's just that since our friend Keiko dumped us to be with the popular group, Vicky's been pretty distrustful. In a way, I don't blame her, but Grace is really fun. She sang in a commercial once, she told me.

"I mean," Vicky said without looking at me, "you've finally lost some of that weight you put on. It looks good."

I laughed a little because I didn't know what to say. Sometimes Vicky gives me a compliment and I want to punch her face.

"So what's new?" I asked.

She took out her tube of Blistex and offered me some. I put it on without really thinking about it. Vicky and I are addicted to Blistex.

"Nothing."

"What?"

"Forget it." She put away her Blistex in her little fanny pack.

"What's wrong?"

"We both know what you want to know. Why don't you just ask?"

"Okay," I said. "Was he there?"

"Yes, and he was wearing a Speedo."

"Oh, gross," I said.

"I mean, leave something to the imagination!"

"Seriously," I said. I wanted to ask her to get off the bed because every time she moved, I ran the risk of barfing again. But I didn't want to hurt her feelings or be a bad host, so I just closed my eyes and tried not to think of a roller coaster. "Did you play?"

"One game," she said.

"And?"

"And what?" She took out her Blistex and put some more on. When she offered it to me again, I wanted to say, No, thanks, the stuff I just put on hasn't even seeped in yet. But it's like an unwritten rule between us—you never refuse an offer of Blistex. I know that sounds stupid, but it has more to do with the give and take of our relationship than with chappage. So I put on more. What the hell. "Well, it's about Grace," she said.

"What about her?"

"She's your friend, forget it."

"What?" Vicky sometimes likes to have things dragged out of her.

"Well, just that if I were somebody's friend, I wouldn't go around flirting with her ex, you know what I mean?"

"She was flirting with Jason? Even though he was wearing a Speedo?"

"Let's just say her bikini got a workout."

I closed my eyes again. "I don't even like him anymore."

"That's not the point. She jumped every time the ball came over the net, and if she fell in the sand one more time, I seriously would've barfed."

"Don't say that word."

"Sorry."

I took off my glasses and covered my face with my hands. Maybe the fever was coming back, because I felt sort of clammy.

"I just thought you should know."

"Okay," I said.

"I would want to know in your position. And you're my best friend, so I felt like I had to say something."

"Thanks."

24

"Don't be mad. Look, I brought you this."

I put down my hands and looked at her. She was holding a red heart-shaped frame with a picture of me and her in it, and around the frame she had shellacked on sparkles and rhinestones and cutouts that said HAPPY BIRTHDAY. The picture was from last summer, the day her mom took us up-island for a birthday picnic the Saturday between my birthday and hers. We were both lying in the grass with our heads propped up on our elbows.

"I made it yesterday," she said, "while Foufhead was over for dinner."

"That bad?" I put my glasses back on because the blurriness wasn't helping my nausea.

"Henry is so *stupid* when she's around. Everything she says, he laughs. Or nods, like she just made such an interesting point. I don't know what he sees in her. Have you ever seen such frizzy hair?"

"Maybe she's really smart. Or nice."

"Yeah, nice. All she does is read and have frizzy hair. Fascinating. Nadine, Nadine. . . He keeps calling her over, even if she's two inches away, and showing her stuff like his old baseball cards, which she pretends is interesting. Yuck, talk about something else. Here." She handed me the frame and put more Blistex on her lips. I thought about saying, Maybe you're jealous, but decided against it.

Instead, I pushed my glasses up on my forehead, took the picture out of her hand, and looked at it closer. We were both tan and smiling, looking a little alike although her hair is less frizzy and her smile is prettier.

"That was before I cut my hair," I said. "I forgot how dopey I looked."

"You looked so pretty," Vicky said, taking the frame back and inspecting. "I look fat."

"You never look fat," I said. "You're still in the eighties, probably."

"Ninety-eight," she said. "But I'm on a diet. If I get into three digits, I'll die."

I held out my hand for the frame again. "Thanks, Vicky."

"I thought it would cheer you up," she said.

"It did," I said. "It is. Hey, you wanna see my new bed?"

I got out of the guest room bed sort of shakily and walked with her down the hall. I was wearing my favorite old flowered leggings, the ones I got last year at a store off-island, and Dad's white T-shirt. I pulled the shirt down in back to cover my butt.

"I mean it, Mol," Vicky said, halfway down the hall. "You look great. You must've lost at least five pounds."

"Six," I said.

I leaned against the door frame while Vicky looked around. "Wow!" she said. "I can't believe it! It looks totally different. It's awesome, Molly. Do you love it?"

"Yeah," I said. "I'm sorry, Vicky. I gotta go to bed."

She turned around and looked at me, and I knew I must've looked not so good because Vicky yelled, "Mrs. Garrett?" and Mom ran up. They helped me back into bed, and Vicky showed Mom the present she had given me. Mom gave Vicky a hug. In the middle I think I must've been dreaming, because I thought they were saying that Abraham Lincoln was really pro-slavery and only issued the Emancipation Proclamation for political reasons. I tried to argue but they had no idea what I was talking about, and after minute neither did I.

Not that much different than usual, only clammier and more historical.

five

I WAS SITTING on the beach wearing my sun hat and new prescription sunglasses, wrapped in my towel because I was still recuperating, thinking how interesting it is that *sun hat* is two words while *sunglasses* is definitely one word, and is that because sunglasses are more common? And also thinking how interesting it is that the opposite of sunglasses is not moonglasses but eyeglasses or just glasses, when Henry sat down in the sand next to my chair.

"Vicky said you were sick."

"I'm mostly better," I said.

"That's good. You been practicing?"

"Some."

"Because you blew off your lesson yesterday."

I was too busy puking to play saxophone was what I thought, and besides, it's too embarrassing to play so badly in front of someone so cute, but what I said was, "Sorry."

He leaned back on his elbows, and we watched the water for a while. "August already," he said.

"Really." I stared at the water. Probably every girl on the beach was wondering what Henry Petowski was doing talking to some mummified kid. Two girls in bikinis strutted right in front of us and smiled at him. He didn't move, so I didn't say anything. I straightened up in my chair a little, though.

"You count, don't you?"

"What?" All I kept thinking was, Please, Vicky and Grace, don't come out of the water yet.

"When you're playing. You know, the beats, the pauses. You count, right?"

"Yeah, I guess," I said. "Aren't you supposed to? I mean, how else do you know how long to pause?"

"I don't know," he said. "You just know."

Vicky walked up from the water with her arms crossed over her chest and her eyes fixed on the sand. She worries that people will judge her in her bathing suit. When she reached us, she grabbed her towel off the foot of my chair and wrapped herself tightly in it. "Hello, Henry," she said, although she was looking right at me.

"Vicky! Wait up!" Grace yelled, running toward us. Vicky rolled her eyes, and I smiled. She hates when people make a scene on the beach, and I knew she was just about dying that Grace had yelled out her name like that. Grace stopped next to Vicky, flipped back her hair, and said, "Whew! God, Vick—was that totally freezing or what?" Vicky didn't budge.

I handed Grace her towel, which was on my lap. She dried her face and smiled at Henry. "Hi," she said. She tightens her eyes when she looks at people—a very attractive habit that I'm trying to pick up. Mom does something like that, too, which may be one key to their popularity, because when either Mom or Grace does that, it makes you feel like she really likes you, really finds you interesting and witty, even if you just said hi.

"Hi," he answered. He pulled in his stomach, I noticed. See? It works. It works. Mental note to practice that in front of the mirror as soon as I'm done writing.

Grace plopped down in the chair next to me. "Ahh," she sighed, smoothing the towel under her.

"That's my chair," Vicky said.

"Does it make a difference?"

"No," Vicky said. "It's just, it's my chair."

"If it's that big a deal, I'll get up," Grace said, lowering the back of the chair so she was almost parallel with the sand. "Is it that big a deal?"

"No," Vicky said. "No big deal. It's just, that's my chair. You could've asked."

"You want my chair?" I asked. "You can have this chair if you want."

"That's not the point. I was talking about *my* chair," Vicky said.

Grace sat up. "If you want it, I'll get up."

"No," Vicky said, shrugging. "That's okay. I don't care." She walked the long way, in front of me and Henry, practically marching, then behind the chairs to the last one in the row. She balled up her towel and threw it down, hard, onto the last chair. She grabbed her beach bag from the bottom of the chair Grace was lying on and took out her sunscreen and slapped it on.

"Oh, can I use some? I think my nose is burning," Grace said.

"It's prescription," Vicky answered. "You better not."

It's just regular from-the-store Almay stuff. I know for a fact, but I was keeping my mouth shut. I reached into my bag and handed Grace my sunscreen.

"Thanks, Molly," she said, with the stress on *Molly*. I felt like a jerk. I didn't want to take sides. It's so complicated sometimes, having two friends. I took off my sunglasses, picked up my book, and started reading again. It's *The Bluest Eye* by Toni Morrison, and so far it's excellent. When I complained one time last year in a moment of weakness about being lonely, Mom said I'd have more friends if I would get my nose out of a book once in a while. I thought of saying, You'd read more books if you would get your ear out of the telephone. I'd never actually say something like that to my mother, though.

"Excellent book."

I squinted up into the sun. Nadine sat down on the foot of my chair. "You've read it?"

"Yeah, I love Toni Morrison," she said. "If you like that, I'll lend you *Beloved.*"

"Okay," I said. "Thanks."

I tightened my eyes at her. She smiled, then stood up and held out her hand to Henry. "Later," he said as they walked away.

"He's after you," Grace said to me.

"That was his girlfriend," I said, putting my sunglasses back on. I watched Nadine and Henry head toward Rocky Bridge, holding hands.

"So what? She had to come get him away from you."

"So," Vicky said, "some people have morals."

"What is that supposed to mean?" Grace asked.

Vicky shrugged and rubbed in her sunscreen.

"He just came over to say I should practice the saxophone more," I said. "Because I stink." I laughed my nervous laugh. It sounded very fake.

"I'm telling you, Molly," Grace said. "I think he likes you."

Vicky threw her bottle of sunscreen in the sand. "Would you *shut up*?" Grace and I both turned to look at her. Her face was all red, and so was her neck. Vicky never says shut up; she's not allowed to. "You don't know him, Grace. You don't know anything about us. You've been here for what, a month? You come here for one month, and you think you're in. You didn't grow up here; you're not like us. One month, and you think you know everything? You can just butt your way in everywhere? Why don't you just shut up? Who the hell are you, anyway?"

"Jeez," Grace said.

"She didn't mean anything, Vicky," I said. "She was just kidding."

"He's my brother. I think I know my own brother a little better than she does."

"Jeez," Grace said again. "What's your problem?"

"No, what's *your* problem?" Vicky stood up and put on her T-shirt. "I'm going for a walk," she said. "Come on, Molly."

"I don't feel that great," I said, picking up my book again.

"Molly," she said in her deepest, quietest voice. I folded down my page, stood up, and pulled the towel around me.

"Be back soon," I said to Grace.

"Whatever," Grace said, pushing back her hair.

Vicky and I went down to the water and turned left, away from Rocky Bridge. Vicky walks so fast, especially when she's pissed, I had to sort of jog every few steps to keep up. My whole life, she's been complaining that I'm too slow a walker.

When we got up to the lifeguard station, Vicky went running into the water and dove in, with her T-shirt on and everything. She's a very graceful swimmer. I sat down on the sand in my towel and watched her swim out pretty far, right through the waves like even they couldn't bother her. Or maybe like they bothered her but she fought them and got through them. Vicky is not somebody you'd want as your enemy. I should warn Grace, maybe. I looked back to the chairs, but I couldn't really see what Grace was doing.

"Hey," Vicky said, dripping over me. She started off in the same direction we'd been going, so I caught up with her. She folded her arms and shivered a little. "How do you stand me?" she asked quietly.

"Vicky."

"I mean it. I don't deserve you."

"Come on," I said. She put her cold arm around me, and we kept walking farther and farther from our chairs.

"What was Henry saying?"

"Nothing. Just hello, I guess."

"Was he talking about Nadine for a change?"

"No. Saxophone."

"She's a slut."

"She seems okay."

"She's a frizz-head and a slut, okay?"

"Okay," I said. She walked in the water; I walked higher, on the packed wet sand. "I'm a frizz-head, too." I was trying to make her laugh. She convinced me last year never to wear a ponytail even if I was boiling by telling me it looked like a raccoon's tail behind me. She didn't laugh, though.

"You shouldn't flirt with him."

"I wasn't! He came up to me! He was talking about my saxophone lessons."

"He thinks you have a crush on him."

"That's ridiculous."

"I just thought you should know."

"Well, it's ridiculous." I pulled the towel closer around me.

"I just didn't want you to make a fool of yourself."

"Thanks," I said. "He said that? He said he thinks I have a crush on him?"

"Yeah," she said. "Don't worry. I told him you don't."

"Thanks," I said again. "Because I don't."

"I know," Vicky said.

We passed by the volleyball net. Some girls from our school were playing. I thought Alissa waved, so I waved back, but she squinted at me like, Who the hell are you? I flicked back my bangs and kept walking.

"Why do we have to hang around Grace all the time?" Vicky whispered. "I can't help it. She just rubs me the wrong way."

"I know," I whispered back. "But she's fun, too, don't you think?" How totally embarrassing: Alissa thinks I wish I were friends with her, and Henry thinks I have a crush on him. Like some dopey little kid.

"You know who she'd be friends with if she lived here? Wendy and Alissa and those girls."

"I don't know."

"Come on, Molly, face it. She's much more like them, all those girls. With their big boobs and flirty, stupid hair flipping. You know she'd be in with them."

"Even if she would," I said.

"And you know what I can't stand? Her butt."

"Her butt?"

"It's so big! She's making an indentation in my chair with it."

I started smiling, so I covered my mouth. My gums show above my braces when I smile. "Come on," I said.

She cracked a smile, too. Her gums don't show because she never had braces. I can't wait to run my tongue over my teeth like the woman in the toothpaste commercial. Two more months.

"Seriously. It hangs out the bottom of her bikini. Haven't you seen her? Yanking it down to cover the vastness of her butt?"

"Everybody does that," I said, hoping it was true. I do it.

"Not like Grace." Vicky imitated her, throwing her hip way out to the side and yanking on her bathing suit. It actually did look a little like Grace. Just a little. I laughed and Vicky started laughing, too. "You know," she said, grabbing my shoulders and shaking me, "you're the only person in the world who can make me laugh when I don't want to?"

I made a nauseated face. She let go and we kept walking, a little slower, so I knew she was feeling better. "Why do you hate her so much?"

Vicky didn't answer right away. She kicked up the sand

in front of her instead.

"I'm sorry," she finally said. "Don't be mad."

"I'm not," I told her.

"Don't hate me, okay?"

"Okay," I said. "Let's head back, okay?"

"I guess," Vicky said, and kicked some sand into the waves. We turned around and started heading back for the chairs. I made a firm decision not to wave at any of those girls, whether they waved at me or not. So what if that's unfriendly. "I mean it, Molly," Vicky said. "Don't hate me. If I lost you as a friend, I don't know what I'd do."

"I couldn't hate you, Vicky. You're my best friend."

six

HOW IS IT POSSIBLE that I will bleed for the next five days in a row and not die?

I wanted this, I had definitely been wanting this all last year. All through eight grade, as soon as anybody got her period, everybody knew. It was like a club, I figured, and I kept praying to join. Grace got hers in sixth grade, she said, but she lives in Manhattan.

So here it is. I'm more like Grace than Vicky now, I was thinking, sitting on the toilet. Maybe the reason Vicky is so nasty to me lately is that somehow she had woman's intuition (can you get that before your period?) that I was finally getting it and about to be more like Grace, leaving her behind, becoming more a woman and less a kid. Woman. Woman. It sounds really stupid if you say it enough times. Woman. I am a woman now.

This is an important moment, I told myself. I pulled up my pajamas and went to my room, which I still haven't slept in, to find my tape recorder. I like to tape-record pivotal moments in my life. When Jason Aronson asked me out last year, I made him repeat it after I got out the tape recorder I had just recently bought. I didn't make him repeat breaking up, though. That was less pivotal, I told myself, and also on the phone, which gives poor resolution. Only the on-the-phone part was true.

I sat on my new bed and pushed the on button. "This is Molly Garrett speaking. I just got my period, finally. It is Thursday, August fifth, at 9:04 A.M. I feel. . ."

Hmm. I feel . . . okay. The same. A little weird, maybe. I guess I got used to writing because it feels more real, now that I'm setting it down on this textured paper. God, it really happened. I got it. Woman woman womanwoman. How do I feel? Sort of, I don't know. A little grossed out, maybe. No, I shouldn't feel that way; that is totally antifeminist. Proud, then. I am proud of my womanhood. Womanwoman. No, I am. It's sort of neat. Wow, I could have a kid. That, if anything, proves I am not a kid myself anymore. Doesn't it? Nature, Mother Nature, thinks I am an adult. Whoa. Who am I to argue with Mother Nature?

I am a woman.

I can't even think that without getting the giggles. Me, a woman. Yeah, that's likely. But I am. This is definitely a pivotal moment. I have to put something on tape. Here goes.

"I feel. . .mixed. About this accomplishment" is what I said. "I am proud to be growing up, proud that my body works right, but maybe a little grossed out that I'm bleeding and also a little sad that I am no longer a child."

The tape recorder is paused, and I'm looking around my room. Very hip, very teenager-y.

"I just hope," I said into the recorder, "I hope my future is as good as my childhood was." *Was*. God. Now there's a final word. My childhood was wonderful, ha-ha, I say to my fiancé, and he calls over the waiter for the check. Ha-ha, ah, youth. Was it? Am I done? What am I going to do with my life?

I put the tape recorder away on the top shelf of my closet. I keep it in a shoe box under Marya Beth, my favorite doll from when I was a kid. I held Marya Beth in my arm while I reached around behind the shoe box for the manila envelope with the books about my changing body. I bought them myself with my allowance in seventh grade. I've already read them a lot of times in preparation, but when I'm tense, I research.

I reread the relevant chapters sitting on my new bed with Marya Beth in my lap. It was the first time I'd really held her since Vicky pulled off her head one day when we were seven, and Mom and Dad sewed it back on slightly crooked. I had to reassure myself that there is a logical reason a human being could bleed for five days and not die, that I am not cut, that in fact there's not that much blood at all. I am sloughing off my uterine lining, I explained to Marya Beth, who looked at me out of the corner of her eye. Gross. Sloughing. Sounds like cows eating. Sloughing off what I don't need to nourish an implanted egg in my uterus, since I'm about as far from getting pregnant as Jason Aronson is. Well, maybe a little bit less far, actually. My body is doing all this stuff without my even trying; it's gearing up, doing what it's supposed to do. It's sort of awesome and empowering, in a way. My uterus. It's mine.

I also wanted to be well informed before I called Mom at The Nail Place to tell her the big news. I knew she'd freak and not be able to hold it in. Then when I got to work, all the ladies would make a scene, bumbling up from where they were sitting at the nail dryers, racing at me with their hands splayed out to avoid denting their polish, making kissy noises and shrieking disgusting things like, Our little girl is growing up. While I was imagining the horror of that, the phone rang. I let the machine pick up because I hadn't decided what to say to Mom yet, but when I heard Vicky's voice, I dropped Marya Beth and the books on the bed and ran into Mom and Dad's room to grab it right away.

"Guess what," I said.

"You got your period."

"Yes! How did you know? Who told you?" For one freaked-out second, I thought maybe somehow the whole island knew already.

"You did?"

"Yeah!"

"Oh, my *God*!"

"But you said, you guessed, you said, 'You got your—'"

"I was *kidding*!" Vicky yelled.

"I wasn't," I said.

"Wow," she said. What I hate about phones is that, exactly. Wow, she said, and even though we've been best friends since she was born (one week after me), I still couldn't tell what she meant. Like, wow, I'm so happy for you? Wow, this means we have nothing in common anymore? Wow, I'm jealous? Wow, you gross me out?

"You're not mad, are you?"

"No."

"But what?" I knew it was something from how she

said no. Sometimes I think it would be easier to be a guy. When Jason gets pissed at Freddy, he says, Freddy, that pissed me off, and maybe even hits him. Maybe they even get in a major fistfight, but then it's right back to armpit farts. Seriously, the worst thing about eighth-grade boys has to be armpit farts. But still, sometimes it would be simpler to be a boy.

"Nothing."

"Vicky, I hate that!"

"Nothing. That's great, congratulations."

"Thanks."

"What did Grace say?"

"What?"

"Was she happy for you, too?"

"I didn't tell her yet."

"Obviously that's a lie."

"Vicky, I just got it!"

"Right, whatever you say."

"I swear!"

"Uh-huh."

"Vicky!" I always seem to be saying the wrong thing to her. Lately my stomach hurts all the time. Maybe I'm blaming Vicky when it was just my period coming. Or maybe I'm being insensitive to her by hanging out with Grace so much. But am I allowed to have only one friend my entire life? Is it betraying Vicky if I also like Grace? Anyway, I didn't tell Grace first. Even if I did, though, wouldn't that be my right? It is *my* period. Then again, Vicky is my best friend, and she feels vulnerable. Everything is so easy for me. I should remember that the same isn't true for Vicky, especially since the thing with her dad leaving, and be a little patient and forgiving and strong.

"Then why did you say, 'Who told you?'"

"Huh?"

"When I guessed it was your period," Vicky said. "You said, 'Who told you?' If you hadn't told anyone else, you wouldn't have asked me that."

"Thank you, Sherlock Holmes," I said.

"Fine," Vicky said, and hung up on me.

I listened to the buzz of the phone for a second and then pressed the button. Damn. I did one of my abrasive screams, since nobody was in the house, then hit the automatic dial for Vicky's number and waited for it to connect. She picked it right up.

"Hello?" She sounded as grown up as anybody's mother on the phone, and like she had no idea who might be calling.

"Vicky," I said.

"Oh, hello, Molly." So cold, I had to be careful not to

touch my tongue to the phone or it would freeze and somebody would have to pee on it. I swear, I heard that on the news last winter about some kid and a flagpole.

"Vicky, I'm sorry."

Nothing.

"I didn't mean to be sarcastic. I know you hate that, and it was unfair of me."

"Whatever."

"You are the only person I told. I swear. I just freaked when you guessed it right away. I haven't even told my mother yet."

"You're not telling your *mother*, are you?"

"No," I said. Vicky doesn't tell her mother anything, on principle. They're not that close. Lots of times I have nothing to say to Mom, either. I don't hate my mother the way Vicky hates hers—I just find it difficult to come up with any topics we're both interested in. I keep thinking we should have heart-to-heart talks and discuss boys and clothes and whatever else mothers and daughters are supposed to have heart-to-hearts about. But if I tell her something, maybe about how I was thinking about thinking about thinking about thinking, she's like, Who are you?

Sometimes Mom looks at me so sad, and I know she's wishing I could be more normal like she is. I've heard her say to Dad, "What am I going to do with her? Where does she come from?" I try to tell her stuff when I can, when I have normal girl things going on, and she really is a good audience. If I'm psyched, she's ecstatic. When Jason broke up with me, she cried, and we baked cookies and ate so much dough we felt sick and skipped dinner. That turned out to be a decent afternoon, considering. So how can I not tell her I got my period? "No way," I said. "She'd get all, you know. . ."

"Seriously. Do you have pads or anything?"

"My mother put some panty liners in the cabinet under the sink a few months ago, hint hint."

"You really didn't tell anybody but me?"

"I swear," I said, crossing my heart even though she couldn't see.

"You're the best," she said. "I'll stop by The Nail Place later and slap you."

"What?"

"It's a tradition. Somebody has to, or the evil spirit will get you, something like that."

"A superstition, you mean," I said.

"Huh?"

"Not a tradition, a superstition."

She said nothing for a few seconds, and then, coldly, "Whatever."

"Thanks, Vicky, that would be great," I said, trying to

sound upbeat so she'd know I hadn't been trying to be obnoxious. "I'd love to be slapped."

Sometimes I get so twisted around, I lose myself in the conversation and end up saying the most asinine things.

seven

WHEN MY PARENTS throw a party, they have to narrow down the list. That's what Mom was doing when I got to The Nail Place at 10:30 on the dot.

"How can I invite the Puccios if I don't invite the Ferrises?" she asked me.

"If you don't want them, don't invite them." I was annoyed with Mom without knowing why. Maybe it was that I couldn't tell her I finally got my period, or because I had been so excited on my birthday to have two whole friends to invite.

"Molly," Mom said, and chewed on her pen. "So maybe I shouldn't have the Ferrises, either, but what about the Galligans? Hi, hon. How was the run?" She kissed me and then wiped my sweat off her lips and her lipstick off my cheek, more or less nullifying the kiss.

"Okay," I said.

I was stretching, leaning on the counter. You have to stretch or your muscles tighten. Also, I didn't want to look Mom in the eye or maybe somehow she'd know about my period. I used to have this fantasy that I'd walk into her room early one morning and she'd be putting on makeup to cover her green witch skin. I guess because she tends to wear pretty much makeup, and also little kids think their mothers can read their minds. Maybe I have a little of that childish feeling left over, like a vestigial organ.

"How fast?" she asked.

"Eighteen minutes." It always takes me eighteen minutes.

"That's great! God, I get winded driving here."

I smiled and Mom smiled back, thinking I was laughing at her joke. I was actually being amused about the other talent I have developed besides stealing. When we learned about vestigial organs in like third grade, I panicked. The teacher told us that humans used to have a tail but lost it evolutionarily through disuse, and that eventually we'd lose our appendixes and pinkie toes. I didn't have any great attachment to my appendix, but

50

the idea of my pinkie toes falling off in my tube socks someday soon freaked me out. I did pinkie toe exercises and taught myself to move my pinkie toes independently from the other toes before I figured out that *evolutionarily* meant pinkie toes weren't coming off for millions of years and I had, therefore, relatively little to worry about.

"Well," Mom said. "I'm gonna check out the polishes that came this morning. You watch the desk?"

"Okay," I said. That's supposedly why she hired me—to watch the desk. I think the real reason is she was afraid if she didn't keep me entertained I'd mope around the house reading all summer. I heard her say that to Dad. If you put your ear against the heat vent in my room, you can hear people talk in the kitchen. She said she wished they could afford to send me to the camp she went to when she was a kid so I'd loosen up and have some fun. A whole bunch of girls sleeping, eating, peeing, doing everything together without a break for two months— camp just doesn't sound that fun to me. I'm sort of happy to work at The Nail Place instead. Mostly what I watch at the front desk is nothing, interrupted occasionally by a customer who needs me to take what she owes out of her wallet for her and sometimes dig her car keys up from the bottom of her pocketbook so she won't smudge her

manicure. It's not bad, but I'd honestly be more entertained reading. Mom and I have a lot of love between us
without understanding each other at all.

"Oh, yes!" Mom yelled. "Candy Apple Red!" She
pulled a bottle of polish out of the carton and looked
right at me but still didn't realize I was a woman. "For
Mrs. Grant. She keeps complaining the Fire Engine Red
is too blue, and really, she's right. Oh, I'm so psyched!"

Sometimes it bothers me when my mother says things
like *psyched*. And that she gets psyched about nail polish.
I should ease up. She tries so hard to relate to me, and,
nice daughter that I am, I don't even tell her I got my
period—which she'd *really* be psyched about. Maybe she's
wrong and I'm not so nice. Just a pinkie-toe-moving car-
keys-digging thief. That'll get me far in life.

She crushed the carton and jammed it into the trash,
then put out the new nail polishes on the stations. "So?"

I looked in the appointment book. "Mrs. Nutik is supposed to be here at ten thirty."

"She's always late. I mean, what's new?"

I shrugged.

"You wanna share a doughnut? Forget it, I shouldn't.
I'm such a cow. But all I had for breakfast was a Tab and
a cigarette. Don't tell Daddy about the cigarette—he'd kill
me."

"Okay," I said. "You shouldn't smoke.. . ."

"I know, I know. I'm definitely quitting today." She reached over the counter to poke the register and pulled out two singles. "Great. And get me a Tab, too, that clear kind. Maybe it's got less junk, I don't know. Is that enough?"

"Plenty," I said. I kissed her and left. Mrs. Nutik pushed past me to get in. Mom winked when I turned back to smile at her.

Mom has been on a diet my entire life. For her birthday last year, Dad bought her a juicer. It's still in the box, but at least she has one. That should count for something, she says. Since Vicky told me the other day I looked better since I lost weight, and said that thing about Grace's butt grossing her out, I haven't been eating much. I have to lose ten pounds immediately, although I object to dieting in general as very antifeminist.

I was standing in line at the doughnut shop, holding a Tab and a club soda and waiting to order Mom's doughnut, when my neck started feeling funny. It doesn't make sense that you'd be able to feel someone staring at you unless telekinesis exists. I really don't believe in all that New Age bull, but when I turned around Jason Aronson was looking right into my eyes.

"Hi," I said, thinking, Why does he always have to see

me when I am a sweaty, disgusting mess? I should've known he would be there—I was looking my worst, after all. If I were ten pounds less, maybe I wouldn't feel like dying. What a stupid thing to think. I'm smart, I'm reasonably well-read for my age, I know how to play "The Hustle" on alto sax, and I can count to ten in five languages. If he can't see past my sweaty, mediocre looks, who needs him?

"Hey," he said. "What's up?"

I never know how to answer that. "Nothing. What's up with you?"

He didn't answer. He rubbed his stomach, which showed under his cutoff T-shirt. Freddy told me last year that Jason does two hundred sit-ups every morning to get nooks and crannies on his stomach.

It was my turn to order. "One chocolate frosted, no jimmies," I said. "It's for my mother," I told Jason. "She hates jimmies."

"Oh," he said, nodding. So what, he was probably thinking. Who asked? I always give too much information. Why can't I ever just *shut up*?

The girl behind the counter handed me the bag. "Oh," I said. "And these." I showed her the drinks and handed her the two dollars. "Well, see ya," I said to Jason.

"Your change," Jason said.

"Oh, yeah." My hair was in my eyes, and I felt very discombobulated. I stuck the change in my sweatshirt pocket.

"Six crullers, please," Jason ordered.

"Well, see ya," I said again.

"Um, Molly?" He took his wallet out of his shorts pocket. It's things like that—he carries his money in a wallet instead of a crumpled-up wad like the other boys—that made me like him in the first place. I guess because it makes him seem more like a man. More grown up. Oh, puke, I am so disgusting. Liking a boy who's shorter than me, wears a Speedo, and has Brillo hair, because he carries a wallet. That is so stupid.

"What? Ow!"

"What?"

"Nothing," I said. Something had grabbed one of my pubic hairs. I am fairly sure it was the panty liner Vicky had told me to put on.

What to do? I can't believe I said *ow*.

"You okay?"

I smiled. "What? Fine. What did you want?"

I tried to very casually change position, shift my weight from one leg to the other, but the thing had a vise grip on me. I put the bag with the doughnut and the two drinks on the counter, which I then leaned on, Joe Cool, as if, while I mentally went over my options. I could stick my hand down my shorts and rearrange. Great. I could try a little plucking action, as if I had a wedgie, from outside my shorts. I could loop my hand up my shorts the way Grace does with her bathing suit and gently give a little tug down. Anything would look disgusting. Maybe if he would take this opportunity to sneeze, I could yank while his eyes were closed. I could just wait and fix myself in the bathroom back at The Nail Place, but I might faint before that and the paramedics would discover the cause of my fainting and, boy, wouldn't the media be all over that.

"Um," he said, handing over a five to the girl behind the counter. "How's Grace?"

"Grace?" I seized the moment to try the wedgie thing, but it didn't work. As he turned back to me, I grabbed the club soda and opened it so he wouldn't suspect.

"Yeah, you know." His eyes are so blue. He counted his change and put it in his wallet.

"Fine," I said. I held up the club soda and said irrelevantly, "This is pretty good stuff, no calories," so he would look at the can while I looped my finger up and yanked down on my underwear. After a sharp stab of pain, relief. My magic lessons last year had paid off; distraction works. Jason took a step closer to me.

"Yeah, well. Tell her I say hi, okay?"

"Uh-huh," I said. He was so close if I puckered we'd be kissing.

"See ya,"

"See ya," I said, and followed him out the door, which he let slam in my face.

"Oh, sorry," he said, after I went, "Oof" or something.

"That's okay."

"Molly?" He rubbed his stomach with the hand not holding his bag of crullers. I told myself that a sane person would find his self-rubbing repulsivo, or at least silly-looking. Not a turn-on. "Could you do me a favor?"

"Sure," I said. Bear your children? I can now, you know. We were walking down Dock Street toward the yacht club, the opposite way from The Nail Place, but Jason is sort of like an undertow to me.

"Find out if Grace likes me?"

"Sure," I think I said. "No problem, gotta go, see ya." I'm not sure what I really said. I just know I said something and then slowly made a U-turn and walked back up the hill to The Nail Place, biting my cuticles. What I meant to say was, What? Find out if one of my best friends likes you? You want me not only to deal that you don't want me anymore, but then I should fix you up with Grace?

I hope you choke on your crullers, Jason Aronson. I hope you end up a male stripper in a sleazy bar, or a drug addict, or a big fat ugly yuck with seven bratty kids and a potbelly that has no nooks or crannies.

eight

"YOU KNOW JASON?"

Grace touched her toes. "Jason?"

"Next four," Ms. Mercer called. She put the CD player back to "Tenth Avenue Freeze-Out" again. It's the worst Bruce Springsteen song. Grace and I crossed with two other girls, doing our turns as we went.

"Focus, Molly! You're not spotting!"

I was totally dizzy by the time we got to the other side, up near the mirror. "Jason Aronson," I whispered, leaning against the wall so I wouldn't topple over.

Vicky wedged herself between me and Grace. "What about him?"

"Oh, the one with the body," Grace said.

"Yeah."

"Next four," Ms. Mercer called. Four more girls twirled toward us. They looked like clods, even Alissa and Wendy. Not as doofy as me, but the Joffrey Ballet wasn't likely to look for new recruits in our class.

"What about him?" Vicky asked again. She had her back to Grace, so I had to look over her shoulder for Grace's reaction.

"Quiet, please," Ms. Mercer said. "Okay, let's go the other way, with the leaps. Back corner, please?"

Everybody groaned. "What do you think of him?" I asked as we all walked to the back of the room. Vicky bent down between me and Grace to adjust her leg warmer.

"I don't know," Grace said. "I guess he's cute, in a scummy kind of way. Why?"

"First four," said Ms. Mercer.

"He wants to know."

"That dick-head!" The music paused just as Vicky said that, and then she had to do a series of four leaps across the floor. She jumped particularly high.

Grace and I were laughing so hard, I could barely get my feet off the floor. I felt like such an oaf, and about as far from graceful as possible. I walked the second half of the way across.

Vicky was staring at me. She spit when she talked.

"He asked you to find out for him?"

"Yeah." I wiped the spit off my face, even though none had actually hit me, but as a way of telling Vicky to cool it. The veins on her neck bulged a little, and I could tell she was pissed at me, not just Jason.

"Oh, he really sucks!"

"It doesn't matter to me," I said.

"Back of the room and sit, please," Ms. Mercer said, clapping. We trudged over.

"Like hell," Vicky said.

Grace whispered, "You went out with him, right?"

I sat against the back wall and pulled my T-shirt down over my butt because the floor is really cold in the dance studio. Grace doesn't wear a T-shirt over her leotard, and you can see her whole bra outlined in the back. Maybe if I lose some more weight, I would stop wearing a T-shirt, but probably not. All I think about lately is losing weight. Today I ate a hard-boiled egg and that can of club soda. I didn't even taste Mom's doughnut. Ten more pounds by school, or maybe twelve. I've gotta get smaller.

"I went out with him for about a minute and a half last year," I said. "I'm totally over it."

"She's not," Vicky said.

"Shut up."

Vicky turned away from me as if I disgusted her. I

61

couldn't help it. She shouldn't pretend she knows who I like better than I do. Anyway, she's the one who told me to break up with him. She said he was obviously only using me for *one thing* and I was making a fool of myself, following him around like a lost puppy who had no other friends. I had some thinking to do, she warned me. But the next day, when I tried to act like I thought she wanted me to, Vicky said if *she* had a boyfriend she would never make a slut of herself the way I had at lunch, coming up to her, Freddy, and Bruce to see if anybody had a pen I could borrow. She said that was a very provocative request and I should've just asked Jason. I had purposely *not* asked Jason to make her happy. I was such a wreck, it was almost a relief when Jason broke up with me. Almost.

But I shouldn't say shut up to her; her mother thinks it's the rudest expression, and although Vicky thinks she's so different from her mother, some things have stuck. Besides, it's just not nice. She was looking out for my best interest. Why do I have to get nasty about it when all she's trying to do is protect me from getting hurt?

"Sorry," I whispered.

She wouldn't look at me.

"Okay, enough," Ms. Mercer said, clapping. She has short-cropped black hair and a British accent, which is probably why she thinks she's so great. That, and her collarbones stick out really prominently, which makes her look strong and fragile at the same time. I think it's a very feminine look, although maybe I shouldn't think that. I'm not sure what I'm supposed to want to look like. I know it's not supposed to matter. That's what adults say to kids who are ugly. That it matters how you look is one of the clearest facts around. My own collarbones are hidden. I've been doing exercises to make them show more.

Ms. Mercer put on some freaky-deaky New Age bogus music and started swaying. We all watched. Her ribs started moving as if they were detached from the rest of her, and her arms trailed along after them. Her eyes were closed. Her head bent to the side, and she sort of spun around it twice; then it looked like somebody loosened all her joint hinges, and she crumpled onto the ground. She stayed there for a minute and then looked up. We didn't know what else to do, so we clapped. Wendy and Alissa started, actually, and the rest of us joined in.

"Free-form interpretation," Ms. Mercer said, sitting on the floor with her legs spread out wide in front of her. "The music fills you. Improv. Pure dance. Who wants to try first?"

Wendy and Alissa looked at each other and giggled. I tried to blend into the floor.

"Wendy, then," Ms. Mercer said. Alissa and Wendy

and Keiko had a total giggle attack. If I ever get that stupid, somebody please shoot me. I'm setting it down in black and white right now so I can't go back on it—if I ever act like that, I will be forced to shoot myself in the kneecaps. I'm glad I'm not popular; giggling seems to be a prerequisite.

Grace leaned over and whispered to me, "If you still like him. . ."

I shook my head like, Don't be ridiculous.

Wendy stood up in front of all of us with her hands over her face. Ms. Mercer put in a new CD. Madonna. "Okay, move," Ms. Mercer said. A whole fresh batch of giggles. Alissa's head was in Keiko's lap, she was laughing so hard. Wendy rocked back and forth with her hips a couple times.

"That's it, but bigger!" The way Ms. Mercer says it, it comes out "biggah." Wendy rocked some more and snapped her fingers a few times. She lowered her head and moved her shoulders a little. I don't like Jason anymore, no matter what Vicky thinks, I kept repeating to myself. If he walked into this room right now, I wouldn't even care. I wouldn't even notice. Well, maybe I'd notice.

"Biggah!"

Wendy spread her feet apart a little and pulled her lower lip over her bottom teeth. Actually she looked pretty good. Wendy has short blond hair and a scar on her chin. I wish I looked more like that, all cute and perky instead of big and lurchy.

"You go, girl!" Alissa yelled out.

"Whew!" Keiko yelled. Keiko does whatever Alissa and Wendy do. Two weeks after Wendy cut her hair to chin length, Keiko cut hers—her long, shiny black hair, her best feature, chopped off to fit in. When she used to be friends with me and Vicky, before we got into sixth grade and discovered who was cool and who wasn't, Keiko used to wear her hair in a ponytail like me. Like I used to. Keiko Chameleon.

"Good," Ms. Mercer said. Wendy sat down next to Alissa, so Alissa jolted her head off Keiko's lap and turned to whisper to Wendy. Sometimes I feel bad for Keiko, because I know deep down she's smart and feels like a fool and wishes (like I sometimes do) that she could come over to my house and we could sit on my stairs and read books the way we used to, but now her self-image is all caught up in being popular. My mother likes Keiko and keeps telling me maybe I should call and invite her over, as if it were that easy. Vicky hates her, thinks she's a traitor.

"Molly," Ms. Mercer said.

"I think I twisted my ankle on that last set of leaps," I said.

"Molly . . ."

I got up and stood where Wendy had stood. If she can do it, I can do it. Ms. Mercer put on the song "I Wanna Fall in Love." I just stood there.

"Let it pass through you," Ms. Mercer said. I looked down. Alissa and Wendy and Keiko were looking up at me, waiting for me to make a fool of myself. Or maybe not. Maybe they empathized and wished me well, and I'm just having a paranoid delusion that popular girls put curses on me. Grace smiled, and I smiled back. Vicky was looking down.

I stood still.

"This music is so . . ." I watched Ms. Mercer search for a word, her body moving fluidly, her head lolling while she made a sound like she was tasting the various word choices. "Juicy."

People started to giggle. I almost started myself.

"Yes, juicy. Give me a dance of juicy."

"Juicy," I said. Grace started laughing out loud, and Alissa's head fell into Wendy's lap. Keiko put her head onto Alissa's hip, but looked awkward. I couldn't move.

"Do your dance of juicy," Ms. Mercer said.

I took a deep breath and started swaying a little, side to side. I even snapped a couple times.

"Biggah," Ms. Mercer yelled. "Juiciah!"

I made a vow to myself right then and there that if I ever have a daughter someday, I will never make her take a dance class ever in her life. She can spend entire summers with her nose in a book, and I will think she's terrific for it. She will never have to perform her Dance of Juicy in front of anyone.

nine

IF I CAN'T have real excitement in my life, I guess anxiety will have to do. I worry that everybody's looking at me. I worry that nobody is looking at me. I worry that I am boring, fat, ugly, not a good enough friend, destined to be an anonymous loser all my life. I worry that it will be hot and I'll sweat uncontrollably and smell or have underarm stains, or that it will rain and my hair will frizz. And that the adults running the country don't know what they're doing, that the democratic process is all just one huge popularity contest, which means not only that I have about zero chance of ever getting to be president, but also that the people in charge of our national security are grown-up versions of popular kids—a terrifying thought when you consider the brainpower and depth of your average popular kid. I worry that at any moment I might make a total fool of myself in front of everybody. I also worry that maybe all these worries are totally realistic.

Henry picked up Vicky in his ice-cream truck after dance class. That's his job for the summer, being the Good Humor Man. He lets me and Vicky get ice cream at his cost, and probably he lets Nadine, too. He's a better saxophone player than businessman. Maybe someday he'll be famous and give me backstage passes to rock concerts he's performing in, and people in the office where I work will say, You know him? and I'll say, Actually he taught me how to play sax when I was just a kid.

When we walked out of dance class and I saw the ice-cream truck, my first thought was, Oh, yuck, I hope he doesn't look at me, because I must look like hell. My next thought was, What if he doesn't look at me because he thinks I am some dopey kid with a completely hopeless crush on him and he's repulsed? And right away, my next thought was, It doesn't make a bit of difference whether he looks at me or not, because he is cool and old and has a college girlfriend I think is beautiful, no matter what Vicky says because she's jealous, and I am his little sister's bumbling, awkward best friend. Face it, the guy does not stay up nights with thoughts of me. Whether he looks or doesn't look is depressingly irrelevant.

"Hey, kiddo," he said when he saw me. Grace bumped into me, and I tripped over my feet. What does it mean that he called me that? Is it a name of affection, like he likes me? Or a way of saying, I think of you as a kid? Or did he just have a momentary mental block against my name?

"Hello, Henry," Vicky said. She still wasn't talking to me since the Shut Up of dance class, so she climbed into the front of Henry's truck and closed the door. Henry made a face at us. He's used to Vicky's moods, and he is the only one, I think, they don't make tense. Vicky rolled down her window and put out her elbow.

"You girls want an ice cream?" Henry asked.

Grace narrowed her eyes at Henry and said, "Whatcha got?"

He smiled and waved his arm at the pictures of ice cream on the side of the truck. "Whatcha want?" Grace blushed and went over to study the pictures. I took off my glasses, hoping the fact that my eyes were unfocused would be overcome by my improved looks. Mom wants me to get contacts, but since I can only read *without* corrective lenses, I'd be poking my finger in my eyes all the time, which is too gross. Maybe I'm getting to the age it's time to deal, though.

"Guess I'll have a Chocolate Eclair," I said.

"You got it," Henry said. "Vicky? Anything?"

"I'm on a diet," she said, and rolled up her window.

Henry shrugged and walked around to the back of the truck, so I followed him. Not like a lost puppy. I mean, he was getting me my ice cream. I didn't have to make him bring it right to me, right? Anyway, I didn't even want an ice cream.

"Maybe I'll have a Bomb Pop instead," I said.

"You're not gonna get all neurotic about your weight now, too, are you?"

I forced a laugh. Heh, heh, me neurotic?

"What's up with her, do you know?" He handed me a Chocolate Eclair. Okay, I told myself. But one hundred jumping jacks and no dinner.

I shrugged and peeled the paper off the ice cream.

"You're coming to her birthday dinner Sunday night, right?"

"Yeah," I said. "I'm sleeping over." Oh, how embarrassing—like I was flirting, like I thought he'd care where I was *sleeping*. So I babbled on: "I don't work on Monday. Any Monday. Because my mom's nail salon is closed." Oh, Molly, why can't you *shut up*?

"I got her a John Coltrane CD," Henry said, politely ignoring my diarrhea of the mouth. "Do you think she'll

71

like that? I didn't know what to get."

"Yeah," I said. "I think that's perfect." Vicky hates jazz, but I didn't want to hurt Henry's feelings or create new opportunities to embarrass myself, chattering. He smiled at me just as Grace came around the side of the truck.

"Oops," she said.

"Did you decide?" I think Henry was blushing. No, definitely not. Why would he blush? I definitely imagined that, probably.

"I'll take a Bomb Pop," Grace said. "You have any money, Molly? I'll pay you back. . . ."

"Sure," I said. Henry stuck his head inside again and found her a Bomb Pop. When he told me $1.50, I knew right away he had charged us both his cost. "Thanks," I said.

"Later," he said as he walked back around the truck. "You don't need a ride, do you?"

"That's okay," I said, just as Grace said, "Sure!"

He smiled that half smile he has and leaned against the truck.

"No, thanks," I said.

"Okay."

As soon as he got in the truck and pulled away, Grace grabbed my wrist. "He definitely likes you. Watch out, girlfriend."

"Shut up," I said. You can say shut up to Grace, she doesn't care.

"Uh-huh. . ."

We started walking toward The Nail Place so Mom could drive us home. Grace lives on North Beach, but Mom doesn't mind. She loves that area, and someday we might move there if The Nail Place takes off and Dad's landscaping business does well. Probably we never will, I guess, but Mom and Dad have been planning to move since I can remember. They used the house-fund money to buy a big-screen TV this spring, though, so it'll be a while, at least.

"I don't really want any more," I said. "You want the rest?"

"Okay," Grace said. She took my Chocolate Eclair with her left hand and alternated bites between it and her Bomb Pop. I've never known anyone before who could bite ices. It's a good thing she has long straight blond hair and such a pretty face, because Grace is my height and weighs probably more than I do. But people look at her. Boys look at her all the time, and even Alissa and Wendy smile at her and laugh at her jokes and stuff. Mom said that Grace has "presence." I have niceness.

"So tell me about Jason," she said with her mouth full.

"I don't know. What you see, you know?"

"Yeah, I hear ya."

"I mean," I said. I say *I mean* a lot, maybe because I rarely know what I mean and I'm constantly trying to figure it out. "He's like, you know, with the walk and all that. . . . I don't know."

"He's bad."

"Yeah, a little."

"Yeah, I know what you mean."

"So do you like him?"

"Not if you don't want me to, I don't."

"Seriously, whatever," I said.

"Why did you dump him?"

"He dumped me."

"Oh," Grace said, and chucked the stick from the Bomb Pop into the street. I had to stop myself from picking it up by weighing the relative worth of saving the environment a tiny bit versus not looking like a jerk. I went with not looking like a jerk. "In that case . . ."

"What?" I asked.

She sucked on the chocolate bar that comes inside the Chocolate Eclair, my favorite part and the reason Chocolate Eclairs are my favorite. Which do I want more, to eat that or to be skinny and gorgeous (redundant?)? I sucked on my lower lip and told myself how pretty I would look by the start of school, in case anybody looked at me. What really got me started on this whole wanting-to-be prettier thing was, I noticed that by the end of last year I was looking over the top of whatever book I was reading at boys more and more, even armpit-fart eighth-grade bozos, but nobody was looking back. And if they ever did, I hid behind the book again. I know my self-worth does not depend on what *they* think, any *they*; still, it would be awfully nice to walk down the halls in the high school and know that people were looking at me and coming up with positive evaluations.

"You want any of this?" Grace held out the stick with the last of the candy. I was about to say no with incredible self-restraint, but then she would've thrown a second stick into the road. So, martyr that I am, I sacrificed my own vanity and did the right thing for the universe. Also, I was going crazy. It was delicious.

"In that case," Grace said, "I say we Billy Mercene him."

"We what?"

"Billy Mercene is this guy in my school at home. He thinks he is the hottest thing, every girl is just dying to go out with him, the whole bit. So me and my friends decided that the next one he hit on would lead him on until he asked her out. Then she'd say, 'No way would I *ever* go out with someone as gross as you.'"

"Did it work?"

"Oh, yeah," she said. "Put him in his place. It was excellent."

I laughed. "That sounds perfect," I said. "Would you really be willing to do that?"

"I'm totally psyched," she said. It doesn't bother me when she says *psyched*. "You wanna go scungilli some stuff?"

"Well, my mom will be waiting for us."

"I thought you said she can't leave till six."

I looked at my watch—5:17. "Yeah, but . . ." I didn't want to scungilli, was the truth. I had made a vow never to do that again. I know, I started it, and it is the only talent I have besides wiggling my pinkie toes independently, and I want to be more of a rebel and not always so vanilla, but last time I threw up for two days afterward out of guilt. The weight I lost as a result was good, but all in all, I'd rather eat less and throw up less. I tossed the stick in a trash can and said, "I don't know."

Grace looked disappointed. How could I say no when she was going to act in such sisterhood with me to put Jason Aronson in his place? I started to smile and she started to smile back. Some things are more important than living a moral life, maybe.

ten

"COME ON," Grace said. "Vicky's right. You walk so slow."

She opened the door to the drugstore and went right up the candy aisle. I really didn't want to steal anything, or to be around her while she did. In rap group last year, the school psychologist told us that when we found ourselves facing uncomfortable peer pressure, we should distance ourselves from the situation. I think she meant emotionally, but I walked up the makeup aisle and looked at the mascara.

It would be easy, I started thinking. Nobody is around me; nobody is looking at me. I took down a mascara and read the information on the back. This brand would make my lashes triple thick. Sounded like a milk shake. Are my eyelashes too thin? I couldn't picture them. I took another type, a lengthening kind, off the rack as if I wanted to compare. I read about triple thickening again or at least looked at each word, but they could've been in Dutch. I slipped the lengthening mascara into my sweatshirt pocket. I think maybe my eyelashes are more of a stubby problem than a wispy problem.

Nothing happened. I put the triple thick back and picked up a waterproof type. So many choices. Meanwhile, my left hand was in my sweatshirt pocket with the lengthening mascara. Maybe it is an addiction: I have a sickness and have to go into therapy. Maybe I should go see the school psychologist when school starts again, and tell her I tried to distance myself but it didn't help. When I went to see her in her office last year after Jason broke up with me, she handed me the whole box of Kleenex. I like that in a person, letting somebody pull her own Kleenex out of the box.

I am good at it, though. I put back the waterproof and went over to Grace in the candy aisle.

She was really pale. "Let's go," she said.

"You okay?"

"Yes," she whispered.

I hiccuped. I get the loudest hiccups in the world.

Grace started laughing, and Mr. Clark looked up from the front counter. I hiccuped again.

"Hold your breath," Mr. Clark yelled from the front of the store.

I held my breath and thought, Stop calling attention to yourself with an unpaid-for lash lengthener in your sweatshirt pocket. I hiccuped again.

"Let's go," I said to Grace.

As we were passing the front desk, Mr. Clark said, "Hold on, girls."

My days are numbered was all I could think. What if Mom and Dad leave me to rot in prison to teach me a lesson? They probably should; it would serve me right. Hiccup.

Mr. Clark took an orange juice from the cooler behind him and poured some into a paper cup. "Drink this," he said. "But pick up the cup with your pinkies and hold your ears with your thumbs and your nose with your pointers."

"What?" Grace had her hands on her hips and was looking at Mr. Clark like he was trying to poison me.

I hiccuped again. They were starting to get caught in my ribs and really hurt. "Trust me," Mr. Clark said. "Surefire cure."

I plugged my ears with my thumbs and squished my nostrils together with my index fingers while Mr. Clark pushed the paper cup toward me on the counter. Just don't let the lengthening mascara fall out of my pocket, I prayed. I hiccuped and Grace and I started laughing, but I only had to remind myself of how close I was to getting a criminal record to focus on the task at hand.

I picked up the cup with my pinkies and bent my knees so I wouldn't have to lean over and take the chance of anything falling out of my pocket. My hands were shaking. I dripped some juice down my sweatshirt but got a little in my mouth.

The cup was back on the counter and I was wiping off my sweatshirt with the paper towel Mr. Clark handed me before I realized my hiccups were gone.

"Hey," I said.

Mr. Clark smiled.

"Thanks."

"No problem," he said.

"What do I owe you for the orange juice?"

"On the house."

"Thank you . . . so much," I said. "I really appreciate it."

Grace and I pushed out onto the street. "God, I feel awful," I said. "He's so nice. I feel so guilty. What did you scungilli? I hope it wasn't too much. The poor old guy probably needs the money to like give to poor hiccuping orphans or something."

Grace bumped into me and smiled. "That was classic," she said. "Truly classic."

I smiled back and pulled the lengthening mascara out of my pocket.

"Awesome," Grace said.

"You can have it," I said. "Knowing me, I'd get conjunctivitis from it."

Grace put it in her pocket. "I couldn't get anything," she said. "He was looking at me the whole time."

"He was not," I said.

She shrugged.

"You never scungillied anything, did you, you big Manhattan faker?" I pushed her away, and she almost crashed into somebody's picket fence.

"So?"

"So, you big faker," I said.

In answer, Grace started singing scales. Seriously. She started low and went up: ah-ah-*ah*-ah-ah. Higher and higher until the windows on the houses we passed started shattering. Not really. But a fat tourist did ride by on a black mountain bike and yell, "Shut up!" in between huffs and puffs. I cracked up. She sang even louder and higher: ah-ah-*ah*-ah-ah.

"You're crazy," I said.

She stopped singing and walking and looked at me

very seriously. "You really think so?"

"Huh?"

"You think I'm crazy? Literally?"

"I was kidding," I said. "I was just kidding." My heart was thumping, I was suddenly so nervous.

"Because sometimes I think maybe I am. Crazy."

"I was just kidding."

"I can't believe you got hiccups," she said.

I took a deep breath. Now I know what not to say, ever, to Grace. People with lots of friends must have to keep files. I smiled at her and tried to think of something, some topic, to make things easier, because I was so tense my knees were about to fall off. "Know what else I got?"

"You got more?"

"No. Something else, something I've been waiting for . . ."

"You did not!"

"This morning," I said.

Grace stopped dead in her tracks again. I thought she was going to freak out again or slap me. "Vicky already slapped me," I said. "So the evil spirit is off."

Grace shook her head and then hugged me. "That's great, Molly. Really. Congratulations."

"Thanks," I said. I almost started crying; I don't know why. It was just so nice, with no making me feel like a jerk for being excited even though she'd already had hers for so long, no being mad that I had said it wrong or not told her soon enough or anything. Nothing. Just congratulations. It was starting to sink in that I really finally got it.

We walked without talking until we reached Hanson Lane.

"So I'll Billy Mercene Jason, right?"

"I guess."

"You still like him, don't you?" She was looking right into me with that tightened-eyes look.

I smiled feebly.

"I'll stay away."

"It's so stupid! He's nasty and obnoxious and arrogant."

"And you can't stop thinking about him."

"And I can't stop thinking about him. I don't know what's wrong with me. The crappier he is to me, the more I love him. It's sick."

"Yup."

I slowed down when we turned onto The Nail Place's block. I wasn't ready to be there yet. "So maybe you *should* Billy Mercene him. It would serve him right."

"No. I'll stay away. Someday he's gonna come crawling to you."

"Yeah, right."

"Mark my words, he will. And you'll blow him off,

because you'll be going out with Henry Petowski."

"Yeah, okay," I said. "And you'll be going out with his best friend."

"Who's even cuter than Henry," she said. "And has wire-rimmed glasses. I love wire-rimmed glasses."

"Really?"

"They are so cool. Some girls in my school get them with clear glass lenses just to be cool."

"Really?" My glasses have wire rims. I thought they were the height of nerdiness. "You wanna try mine on?"

"Yeah." We sat down on the sidewalk outside The Nail Place, without saying anything. We sat at the exact same second. "It's an omen," she said, taking the glasses from my hand and putting them on. She was blurry to me, but actually she looked sort of cool and intellectual in my glasses.

I felt really okay about everything, really clear. The haze of the morning had burned off and the late afternoon sun felt great on my head, the air smelled thick and August-y, I had my period. I closed my eyes and leaned my head against the window behind me. Everything was basically right.

"Thanks," Grace said. "For the mascara, I mean."

"No problem," I said. "Don't mention it. To anybody."

She laughed. I didn't even care that we were so bad,

that I had done it again after I had sworn not to. It seemed okay, like we were in it together, so it was more like a rite of passage. I wasn't even embarrassed that I had told her I still liked Jason. We just sat there for a while and didn't have to say a word to each other.

eleven

SINCE MY BIRTHDAY, I've lost eight and a half pounds. Eight and a half pounds in six days. Not bad. After I got on the scale this morning, I felt really terrific, really in control. I think my period went away, though. I thought it was supposed to go on for a while, like five days. What if it was a false alarm? What if I'm not a woman, after all that? Good thing I didn't mention anything to Mom, I guess. I've also developed a new method for getting laryngitis. It's sort of an extended throat-clearing thing, which is better than screaming since it's quiet enough to do when other people are in the house. I may be sounding sexier already.

It was raining really hard, so I took a ride with Mom to The Nail Place instead of jogging and just stayed there with

Mom all afternoon. Mrs. Puccio complimented me on how I looked, and asked if I had lost weight. I don't know, a little, I said. As if. I know to the ounce, and how much more to go. But that put me in a good mood, too, and when Soraya asked if I wanted her to do my nails, I said yes and let her do a French manicure and even trim my disgusting cuticles. She mentioned that my voice sounded sexy and asked if I had a sore throat. Maybe I'm getting to be less tough and more feminine now that I've got my period. I definitely got it, I decided. That wasn't my imagination. Maybe the first time is just a little, with some people. I'll have to reread the relevant chapters in my books.

After work, Mom and I went to the Gap and picked out a shirt Mom said Vicky would love for a birthday present. Pretty boring, but I didn't know what else to get her. Mom also bought me two new pairs of socks, one orange and one green. I like wacky socks. It made me feel that much guiltier about not telling her my news, having those new socks in the bag just for nothing, just because I like wacky socks and Mom knows it. I almost decided, screw Vicky, I'm telling my mother, but we were home before I spit it out, and Mom had all those people to call and invite to her dinner party. The rain had stopped and everything outside smelled delicious. I took *The Bluest Eye* from my new night table and dried off the porch swing so I could sit out there and read instead of practicing my saxophone, to get back at Henry for thinking I had a crush on him.

Dad drove up in his truck a few minutes after I finished the last chapter, so as far as he could tell, I was just sitting on the porch swing, lost in space as usual, when in reality I was letting the book seep into me. My father never just sits and thinks; he's always working on something. I think he's just as weirded out by me as Mom is, if not more. He came up on the porch and sat on the step, facing away from me out toward the garden, pulling weeds from the cracks in the steps. He seriously hasn't looked at me since my boobs started growing. Although I always hated being tickled, it's sort of lousy that he doesn't ever anymore. Who'd have thought I would miss that?

We sat there for a while until he was done pulling out all the weeds. I watched him, so meticulous, not missing a single one, and yanking all the roots out each time. He's so careful. I'm always a mess, doing three things at once or doing nothing at all. He's not a bad-looking man, tall and thin, his jeans sagging way down beneath his lack of butt.

He stood up and, still facing away from me, said, "I'm gonna get some 'hogs, make some soup." When I was nine, we had a nanny, this really fun college girl named

Pauline Ames, who almost freaked and left the first night here because she didn't know 'hogs were quahogs (clams), and she thought Dad was going to shoot a pig for pork soup. It's been a family joke since then.

"Can I come?" I hate going clamming. It's smelly and gross and the quahogs spit at you. I don't know if Dad was happy or not that I asked to come. It's hard to tell with him because his only real facial expression is squinting, which he uses for every emotion.

He squinted at me for a second, maybe to see if I was serious. "Sure," he said, and walked out to the toolshed.

I ran upstairs to change into cruddier clothes and grab my tape recorder while he was putting the basket and shovels into the truck. I thought I might have a pivotal moment with Dad while we were clamming, and I didn't want to miss taping it. Maybe what I've been missing is some quality time with him. I raced down the stairs, thinking about a day when I was little and he took me out clamming. On the way, we stopped and bought a big wood-and-paper glider, and we spent hours playing with it before we realized it was getting dark and we hadn't dug a single 'hog. I can picture him hoisting me up onto his shoulders with the glider in my hand, running down the rocky bank of Quinsocket Pond, yelling, "Now! Now!" and me being afraid to let go of the glider because I knew

I couldn't get it to do loop-the-loops like when he held it. That was one of my top ten days. He kept laughing. "You gotta let go, Minute! You gotta let it fly!"

Maybe my enchanted spot is out at Quinsocket Pond with Dad, and I just never realized.

I hiked myself up into Dad's truck and slammed the door shut. It smelled like potting soil and newsprint and black coffee in the cab, just like in his old brown truck. That was reassuring. I was feeling good about going with him. He said, "I'll be right back," and took the porch steps two at a time to go in and, I guess, get something or tell Mom goodbye. I put my feet up on the dash.

When Dad had the brown truck, Mom always used to bug him to wash it, but since he had told me the only thing holding that old truck together was the dirt, I thought Mom was plotting its destruction. I knew she hated it, which made me love it and feel like only I really loved Dad and would defend him. I liked how the floor crunched when you stepped on it, and I liked the rubber bands from the newspaper hanging around the radio dial. Even though I was frightened to be in that truck when it rained because I believed Dad when he said that about the dirt, I usually felt terrific riding in it. Felt like Daddy's little princess, high up above all the ordinary cars.

While I was remembering all that, Dad yanked open

his door, which made me jump. He said, "Sorry," and I said it was okay. The radio blared when he turned on the engine, so he lowered the volume and we bumped down out dirt road. Grace thinks it's very sweet and rustic that I live on a dirt road. Lots of people have dirt roads on the Island; I never noticed it, really.

A Joe Cocker song came on right as we hit the main road. I turned it up, and Dad and I sang along. He didn't know any of the lyrics but he sang anyway, making up his own as he went along. I have to admit this sort of bugged me, although I admired his ease with himself. I could never make up nonsense lyrics as I went along. I feel so ashamed when I sing the wrong word or start the wrong verse. I hate making mistakes. Dad doesn't mind. We drove down toward Quinsocket, him singing random lyrics and me singing the real ones, with his arm not around me but sort of on the back of the seat.

"Maybe we should stop off at Clark's and get a glider," I said, smiling at him.

"What?"

"Remember that time you got me a glider? And we flew it down at Quinsocket?"

He shook his head.

"I was a little kid, remember? Come on, you remember. You made it do loop-the-loops, and I could only make it crash into the sand?"

"Sorry," he said. "Don't remember. What's wrong with your voice?"

"Nothing. I'm losing it."

We unloaded all our gear at the end of Quinsocket Road. Dad walked toward the pond carrying everything but my little shovel and rake, left over from when he bought them for me back I don't know when. I picked them up and followed him down the hill. By the time I got to the edge, he was already well into the water, with the basket tied to his waist and floating beside him in its inner tube like an obedient pet. I poked at the sand, then turned on my tape recorder.

"Hey, Dad?"

"Yeah?"

"When you were my age, had you already started drinking and everything?"

"Yup," he said, squinting at the water. My father is a recovering alcoholic, which is why he looks older than he is. You say *recovering* even though he hasn't had a drop in over ten years, because he'll always be recovering, never completely cured. That's what Mom told me.

"You were pretty wild when you were my age, huh, Dad?"

He nodded. I thought maybe he would tell me what it

had been like being the bad boy, the one all the girls wanted and Mom got. That's what Mom said he was like. I can't picture Dad being so wild, although all the women still seem to like him, so maybe. I tried to wait for him to start talking, but minutes passed and it became clear that he'd need to be prodded.

"What made you fall in love with Mom?" I imagined him saying something like, Because she was as beautiful as you are right now, Minute. I realize that's farfetched, but it would've been really nice.

"Lighten up, huh, Mol? Get some 'hogs."

I leaned on my shovel and watched him clamming while the sun set behind him, and attempted to figure out something meaningful. What am I going to do with my life? I taped the silence between me and Dad, waiting for something to happen. I knew a half hour had passed when the tape clicked off. I stuck the shovel in the sand and got spit at by a quahog, which I let sit on the shovel until Dad waded out and threw it on top of his bucketful and said, "Let's go."

We rode home with the radio off, and when we got to the house, I went straight upstairs without helping unload the gear. I labeled the tape PIVOTAL MOMENT WITH DAD and put it in the shoe box under my old doll Marya Beth with all the others.

twelve

VICKY HELPED ME pick out what to wear to her party. I was thinking I would wear my pink top from New England Knits with white pants, but Vicky said you can't wear white pants, while you have your period. I told her I think it's done, but she said, No reason to ask for trouble—it could come back. And the pink top with jeans made me look a little chunky, she said, no offense, ha-ha. Karen Carpenter, some singer from the sixties, got anorexia and starved herself to death after a reviewer mentioned she looked a little chunky. I whipped off the pink top and put on my big black cotton sweater and black leggings with the orange socks Mom had bought me, and the gold bracelet from Grace. Vicky thought that was a cute look, and by then I didn't really care. It was her birth-day—whatever made her happy.

I left her sitting on my new platform bed while I went to the bathroom. I took my time, more because I needed to be alone than for any feminine reasons. We had spent the afternoon at the volleyball game down at Alora Beach, and Jason had on his normal red-white-and-blue shorts instead of a Speedo. He looked hot, I have to admit, all dark with those blue eyes. I was on his team for one game and we smashed into each other going for the ball at the same time, so we ended up in the sand and lost the point. He laughed; I was mortified. I inspected my knees for scrapes that weren't there and cursed myself silently for being such a clod.

I was spacing out on the toilet, wishing that I had brought my journal in with me or that I could think of a way to ask Vicky to go downstairs with my mother and watch Oprah for a few minutes so I could write. It was on my night table, where I left it after I showed Vicky I really am writing in it, because she didn't believe me and thought I hated her present. Not that I think Vicky would read it or anything. I trust her. I just wanted to write in it like I'm doing now and try to sort out how I felt about Grace flirting with Jason all afternoon.

There's nothing I can do now about having smashed

into him; it's too late. I never should've gone for that ball, or I should've at some point in the past developed my peripheral vision so that I could have seen him coming and pulled back, but the only choices left to me now are to feel bad or not to. Or I guess, additionally, to try to convince myself it never happened.

It's *now* for so short a time, a totally uncatchable time, because as soon as the thought has crossed my mind, "This is *now*," it's too late; I have already thought that thought in the past. It makes me dizzy. One thing leads backward to the next, and it's hard to figure out where everything started. I wouldn't have gone for that ball and made a fool of myself if Grace hadn't been serving right at Jason all afternoon, pissing me off because she promised she would stay away from him. And she wouldn't even have been at the game if we weren't friends, which we wouldn't be if either she or I hadn't gone to the arcade on the Fourth of July, back when she had nobody to hang around with except her little sister, Simone. If I had decided to stay home that day and read a book instead of letting Vicky drag me to the arcade, I wouldn't have ended up looking like a dork in front of Jason.

Maybe that's ridiculous, but it's what I was thinking, and the whole chain-of-events logic made me feel paralyzed, like any move I made could be so impactful it would change the whole course of my life. So I sat there on the toilet for I don't know how long, until I convinced myself that that was a decision, too, with the probable next event being that Vicky would think I had diarrhea or something.

When I went back into my room, Vicky was lying down on the bed. She watched while I put stuff into my backpack—my Garrett Landscaping sweatshirt, extra panty liners (just in case of Revenge of the Period), shorts, my journal. I knew I wouldn't have any private time at the sleepover, but I didn't want to hurt her feelings or make her think I hated her present by not bringing it.

Mom drove us over to Vicky's at around six and convinced Vicky to open her present in the car. I leaned forward from the backseat to watch. As she pulled out the shirt from the big white Gap box, Vicky went, "Oooo," and held it up to her. "Thanks," she said, and kissed Mom.

"I hope it's the right size," Mom said. "You're so petite!"

"I'm sure it is," Vicky said, and turned around to kiss me. I leaned way into the front so she could, and then we got out. We went straight up to Vicky's room, where she put the box on her bedspread. Vicky has a bedspread instead of a comforter. Every morning she makes her bed look as good as a bed in the Conran's catalog.

"Aren't you going to try it on?"

"Maybe later," she said.

"Maybe you could wear it for your birthday dinner tonight. . . ."

"Well, even if it does fit, I have to wash it first, right?"

"Oh, yeah," I said. I don't wash everything first, but I wasn't about to say anything. What did I care if she liked it or not? She could return it. I wish I'd thought of something better to get her.

When Grace got there around six-thirty, Vicky was sitting on her bed polishing her toenails, and I was leaning against the dresser thumbing through her *Cosmo* magazine. Vicky won't put her feet on the bedspread itself—even if she's not polishing her toenails, she always puts a small white towel under her feet. I just sit on the floor. Grace sat down on the edge of Vicky's bed, and Vicky caught the tipping nail polish bottle just in time.

"Careful!"

"Sorry," Grace said, and dropped a small box on the bed next to Vicky. "Wasn't volleyball fun today?"

I shrugged and pretended to care about tips for making your hair shinier. "Look," I said, pointing at the magazine. "We should crack eggs over each other's heads!"

"What's wrong with your voice?" Grace asked. I didn't

say anything, just smiled inside myself that the change was getting noticeable.

Vicky closed her bottle of polish, opened the box, and pulled out a gold bangle. "Thanks," she said, and put it right on.

Grace gave her a kiss on the cheek. "Hope you like it."

"I adore it," Vicky said. I couldn't help looking at the chain around my wrist and wondering which was nicer, mine or hers, and if it meant something that Grace gave Vicky a bangle instead. I'm embrassed that I'm petty like that, but I have to write it down because I did promise to report the truth, even the bad parts. If people knew the truth about me, they'd probably hate me.

"Girls? Dinner," Mrs. Petowski yelled up.

"Coming!" Vicky put all her pedicure equipment back in her Lucite container, which she carried over to her desk, walking with her toes as splayed out as possible. Of course, she doesn't know how to move her pinkie toes independently. She was the last of us down to the dining room.

The table was set with a really pretty white lace tablecloth, and Mrs. Petowski, Henry, and Nadine were already sitting at the table, all smiling up at Vicky. She sat at the head of the table facing her mother, I sat next to her, and Grace sat between me and Mrs. Petowski, across from Henry.

"Clam chowder?" Vicky frowned at her bowl.

I took a taste. I knew it was the bought kind, which doesn't compare to Dad's but I said something like, Mmm, delicious, to try to ease what was going on.

"For my birthday dinner? Thanks a whole heck of a lot, Mom."

"What's wrong with clam chowder?" Grace asked. "I thought all you Leewarders were like really into it."

"I hate food that floats," Vicky said without opening her mouth.

"Really?" Nadine leaned toward Vicky. I smiled across the table at her. She was wearing a pretty floral sundress, and her hair was in a loose French braid with some pieces hanging down. Maybe I should learn to do that with my hair when it grows out.

"Really," Vicky said, her hands still in her lap, still staring at her mother. When she looks at me that way, I feel like my skin is melting right off my skeleton. "And you know it, Mom."

"All foods that float?" Nadine leaned her head on her hands. She and Grace were all interested, not knowing the warning signs to crawl under the table and hide, at least figuratively.

"Vicky, let's not have a scene, please," Mrs. Petowski said, and took a spoonful of soup. Mrs. Petowski looks like Cruella de Vil from *101 Dalmatians*, so I was frightened of her when I was little. She has the longest, thinnest fingers—very elegant, as if she should be in Vienna or someplace fancier than the Island.

"Like cereal?" Nadine asked. Vicky nodded without taking her eyes off her mother, who was eating her soup very delicately. I decided excusing myself to go to the bathroom would draw more attention to me than doing nothing. I couldn't decide which would be better: to eat or not to eat.

"So if there were just broth, that would be fine?" Grace asked. Vicky nodded. Grace and Nadine smiled at each other.

"I finished *The Bluest Eye*," I told Nadine. I thought maybe it would diffuse the situation if I changed the subject, and also I guess maybe I didn't want an alliance to form between Grace and Nadine without me. It didn't work, though. My comment was left stranded, hanging over the table randomly. Nadine was too intrigued by Vicky's food weirdness to be distracted by me.

She looked at Vicky. "So why don't you just avoid the floating stuff and eat the broth?" Vicky ignored Nadine, except that a muscle tightened in her jaw. Henry finished his chowder and sat back in his chair.

"How about fish?" Nadine asked. A relevant question

I had never asked Vicky. I looked at her. She pushed her bowl into the middle of the table. I took another spoonful. Nadine hadn't touched hers yet. "That's so interesting. I never heard of that."

"She hates condiments, too," I said, and everybody looked at me like I was a lunatic. "You know, ketchup, mayonnaise. Mustard totally grosses her out."

"Really?" Nadine nodded at me and tasted her soup, or at least put some in her mouth. I don't think she noticed it one way or the other. "It's so interesting, female food phobias. Girls grow up so weird about food, don't you think?"

"I guess," I said.

Mrs. Petowski cleared the bowls and went through the swinging door into the kitchen.

"I like everything," Henry said.

"That's just my point," Nadine answered. Grace and I were totally into her. "Why are girls so freaked out by food? Like do you know exactly what you weigh?" Grace and I both nodded. I didn't think Grace would; she never seemed to care that much what she ate. Vicky didn't look up from the tablecloth, but I know she always knows to the half pound. "So do I," Nadine said. "And I used to have weird gross-outs, too, like I couldn't stand to let a fork touch my teeth. Gave me chills."

Vicky jerked her head up and looked at Nadine before she could stop herself, but looked back down right away.

"You, too?" Nadine asked her. Vicky nodded once, barely. "Isn't that weird? What happened to us all that we got to be such a wreck?"

"I hate ice cubes," I said. I wished I hadn't, because I realized too late that we were done cataloging weird phobias and were on to drawing some kind of conclusion. Nadine said uh-huh or something but didn't really pay attention or ask me to elaborate, which I could have, because I really can't stand ice cubes clattering against my teeth, especially since I got braces. But nobody seemed particularly impressed.

Vicky's mother came back into the dining room with a big platter of pasta primavera, Vicky's favorite. She should have smiled at Vicky to show she had made it especially for her, but she didn't. She just plunked it down on the table and handed Henry the spaghetti scooper. He served some to Nadine, who was not any more interested in spaghetti than in clam chowder.

"It's like we have no internal certitude, you know?" Nadine said. I don't think Grace had a clue either, but we both nodded. "Like we have to create all these constructs, these rules of weirdness, and go against every instinct for survival until we've obliterated any instincts at all, because we have no inner serenity."

Henry plopped some spaghetti on his mother's plate, and she said thank you. Usually at Vicky's house, there's not this much talking at the table, and any that there is is all just polite. Grace and I kept nodding, even though we didn't know exactly what we were agreeing with. It sounded so right. Henry passed me the scooper after he served himself. I served Vicky and myself, me a slightly smaller portion, which Vicky noticed, so I knew it would be a competition of who could eat less.

"Delicious," Henry said with his mouth full.

"Good," said Mrs. Petowski. "I'm glad you like it."

Nadine's eyes were bugging out. "I had this one woman, she had a wide-open chest wound."

"Nadine volunteered in a hospital last semester," Henry explained. I think Nadine sometimes makes him nervous. Weird that it would be Nadine and not Vicky, the opposite of my reaction. Nadine makes me feel like I can't wait to grow up and go to college and stay up all night talking about God and eating pizza.

"How interesting," Mrs. Petowski said. She poured a little salt on her plate from a crystal salt-shaker she held very high above the table. She looks aristocratic shaking salt. "Are you premed?"

"Possibly," Nadine said. "She had this wide-open

wound, this obese woman, and she couldn't get comfortable anywhere but on the toilet."

"Nadine," Henry said. Grace and I tried not to smile.

"So I'd go in with her breakfast tray or whatever, some flowers, and she'd be in the bathroom, like, 'Come in, come in. Don't be shy.'"

"I'd freak," Grace said, gobbling up her spaghetti. I ate some and put down my fork while I chewed.

"Is your father a doctor?" Mrs. Petowski asked.

"Mother and father," Nadine answered.

"Did you go in?" I asked.

"I'd run," Grace said.

"Yeah, I talked to her a lot. I really liked her. She was so beautiful."

"An obese woman on a toilet with a wide-open chest wound was beautiful?" Henry almost choked on his pasta.

"That's such a male attitude. Yes, she was beautiful. She had on these earrings, the dangly kind, you know, with the fake rhinestones?"

I nodded.

"As opposed to real rhinestones," Grace said, smiling.

"Shut up, Grace," Nadine said, with a smile right back like they were old pals.

Mrs. Petowski took a loud breath. "Pass the Parmesan, please," she said.

"So she'd shake her head when she talked to me until I complimented her earrings. She was much more interested in talking about the earrings than in the fact that she was dying. She didn't seem scared or anything. *She* had a great survival instinct."

"Could you see right into her chest?" Grace asked. "Like, her innards?"

The corners of Vicky's mouth sank down.

"That's not the point," Nadine answered. "What I mean is, don't you think it's significant of something that our generation is lacking? This woman was dying from a wide-open chest wound, and she was proud of her earrings."

"I think that was a disgusting story," Vicky said, and pushed her plate away. I had eaten more than she had. She stood up. "Thank you for ruining my birthday dinner, Nadine. And Grace." She took off her new bangle and dropped it on the table, then walked slowly up the stairs and slammed her door shut.

"What did I do?" Grace yelled after her.

"I'm so sorry," Nadine said. "I didn't mean . . ."

"Don't worry about it," Henry said. "Vicky torques out over everything."

"Should I go up?" I asked Mrs. Petowski while she and I cleared the dinner plates.

"Absolutely not," she said. I went back and sat at the table and listened to Henry talk about John Coltrane. He opened the CD he'd bought for Vicky's present and put it on.

Mrs. Petowski made him turn it off when she brought out a beautiful birthday cake with HAPPY BIRTHDAY VICKY in pink icing and fifteen candles blazing (one for good luck). We sang loud so Vicky would hear us, and we all blew out her candles for her.

thirteen

I WENT UP to Vicky's room when everybody was done eating cake and knocked on her door.

"Go away," she growled. I pushed open the door—she's not allowed to have a lock on it. She shot up from where she was sitting on the bed and flew at me, yelling, "I said leave me alone!"

I backed away right into the door, which slammed shut, but she had grabbed on to my hair. I felt part of my head get torn away.

"Ow," I think I said. She had a wad of my hair clenched in her fist. I couldn't take my eyes off it. I pressed my hand against the burning part of my scalp and tried to breathe.

"Don't betray me," she said, really low.

"I didn't. I won't." My scalp was throbbing. I wanted to check the mirror to see if there was a bald spot under my fingers, but I couldn't move.

She started to cry. "Yes, you will."

"I won't, Vicky." I took my hand off my head and put my arms around her. She was bawling.

"No matter what?"

"No matter what. But you gotta leave my hair alone."

She laughed and pulled away to look at the hair in her fist. "I'm sorry," she said. She went over to her garbage can and brushed off the hair into it. "I just felt like everybody was turning on me, even you."

"I wasn't."

"Because if you ever betray me, you'll regret it."

I sat down in her desk chair because my head felt funny and I thought I might throw up my dinner. I was glad I hadn't eaten any cake. "I wouldn't," I said, checking my scalp in the mirror. No bald spot.

"Is Nadine gone?"

"Yeah." Henry was driving her home, but I didn't think I needed to mention that. She had given me her copy of *Beloved* before she left, and told me I should call her when I finished.

"How about Grace?"

"She's downstairs. She wants to call her housekeeper to pick her up."

"Good," Vicky said. "She ruined my birthday."

"No, she didn't."

"Not as much as Nadine, but she helped." Vicky dropped the Gap box with the shirt I had bought her on the floor and sat on her bed.

"Come on, Vicky—for me? Make up with her."

"Did she ask you to come up and talk to me?"

"No," I said. "I just . . ."

"If you want me to," she said.

I was surprised it was that easy, but sometimes Vicky just needs a little reassurance that I'm on her side. I went down and, after a lot of persuasion, got Grace to go up to Vicky's bedroom and say, "I'm sorry if I did something wrong" (the if because she didn't think she actually had), and Vicky accepted that. Grace held out the gold bangle and Vicky put it on. Maybe I'll work at the UN.

It was already midnight, so we turned out the lights, went to bed, and talked—at least till I fell asleep—about what we think will be the most important issue facing our generation when we grow up. I couldn't think of one, I had such a thumping headache.

When I woke up at about three in the morning, Grace was gone. I put on my glasses and looked out Vicky's window over her desk, and saw Grace walking around in the backyard. I threw on my sweatshirt but no shoes and went out to see what was wrong. She was picking dandelions and blowing the white stuff away, making wishes and crying, and keeping the stems in a bouquet.

"What's up?" I asked, even though I hate that question.

She wiped her nose with the back of her hand. "Nothing. Allergies." She bent down and blew another dandelion white away.

"Then why are you picking dandelions?"

"This kid in my school? He heard you get a wish if an eyelash falls out, right? He pulled out all his eyelashes."

"Gross."

"I swear."

"I believe you," I said. "It's just gross."

"Don't tell anybody what I told you about last night, okay?"

"Okay," I said. I think maybe I was asleep when she told me, because I couldn't remember anything she said that could be so private. She thought universal health care would be the major issue, but that's not such a big deal. Why didn't I just say, What thing you told me about? But my impulse is to lie, I guess. That's a really bad trait of mine.

"You don't think Vicky will say anything, do you?"

"No," I said. "Don't worry."

"I think she might have been asleep, anyway."

"Yeah, maybe." I pulled the tube of Blistex out of my sweatshirt pocket and held it out to her. She took some and so did I. Grace had never used Blistex before this summer, and I don't think she likes it that much, but I guess she figured out without me or Vicky saying anything that you always just take it when it's offered, as a friendship thing. That's what's great about Grace—she understands stuff without needing an explanation.

"You wanna come with me to England?"

"Huh?" I asked. "When?"

"When I run away to open the Home for Stray Dogs and Kids," she said. "In a few years. Were you asleep, too?"

"No," I lied again. "I just thought maybe you meant something else. I wasn't sleeping."

"Then you'll go?"

"Okay." I screwed the cap back on the Blistex and put it in my pocket. It's that blast of cold you get when you put it on that has me addicted. It hurts a little, but it feels good at the same time. I am a sicko.

"Vicky could come, too, if she stops hating me."

"She doesn't hate you. She just gets like that sometimes. You have to be patient with her. She's really a good friend, down deep. And she loves dogs."

"Well, she can come to London with us if she wants. But don't say anything to anybody, or the whole thing will be messed up."

"Okay," I said. "Hey, you didn't tell anybody about scungilli, did you?"

She shook her head. "Who would I tell?"

"Don't tell anybody, okay? Not even Vicky. She wouldn't, I mean . . . I just, it's not worth . . ."

"Okay. Thanks." She smiled and wiped her nose again. She thought I was saying it just so we'd be even and have to trust each other, I guess. That was only part of it.

I nodded. "You wanna go to bed?"

"I'm not really that tired. Are you?"

"Yeah," I said. I rubbed my eyes under my glasses to show her how tired I was.

"I don't know how you can sleep. Look at those stars— see that? That's Jupiter."

I looked up. "Really? Jupiter?"

"You can tell because it doesn't twinkle. See? Planets stay solid."

"I didn't know that."

"Yeah. I learned about it in the planetarium. I never see stars or planets or anything for real at home, because it never gets dark in Manhattan. I don't want to waste my chance."

"Okay," I said again, and yawned. "I'm going back to bed."

As I was walking away, she blew a dandelion white. "I don't know how you can sleep with this sky."

In the morning when I woke up, Grace was reading *Cosmo* and Vicky was still asleep. My journal was on the floor, so I put it away in my backpack. I didn't want Vicky to be mad that I was mistreating it or something. I read *Beloved* until Vicky woke up, and then we all brushed our teeth together. Grace and Vicky both laughed when I drooled toothpaste down my chin. It didn't bother me. Afterward we went into Vicky's room and described what our weddings would be like someday. Vicky and I are going to be each other's best woman (*maid of honor* sounds like you have to vacuum), and although Grace will have to have Simone, she said Vicky and I could be bridesmaids or other significant women. Vicky wants it to start snowing just as she's saying "I do."

Mrs. Petowski yelled up that she was running to the store for orange juice, because somehow there was none left. "Okay," Grace yelled down. Vicky laughed instead of getting mad that it was her house, her mother, her place to say okay. Writing it down like this makes me realize how many unspoken rules there are with Vicky. No wonder I'm tense all the time. So much to remember about what not to say and how not to act. Maybe if I just ignored the rules, Vicky would lighten up. More likely she would stop talking to me, and things would be even tenser. Not worth it. I have to prove to Vicky that not everyone will abandon her, just because she feels that Keiko did and her dad did. I won't So I follow all her little rules. No big deal.

Grace pulled a pack of cigarettes out of her bag as soon as Mrs. Petowski closed the front door.

I looked back and forth between Vicky and Grace, thinking, This is it—now Vicky is kicking Grace out for sure. Vicky and I both hate smoking; it is the most vile thing in the world, and I see absolutely no positives in trying it. Either it would be as disgusting as it seems or you might like it, and then you'd spend your shortened life smelling bad, with yellow teeth and fingers, until you died an ugly, painful death.

"Let's go in the bathroom," Vicky said, looking right at me. I couldn't believe it. After Mr. Petowski moved out, Mrs. Petowski started smoking those long brown cigarettes and Vicky said it was repulsivo, something she would never ever do. We've been on a serious campaign to get our mothers to stop killing themselves with smoke.

"Vicky . . . ," I said, trying to get her to think.

She had already started out her bedroom door, but she turned around and gave me a look as if I had some hell of a nerve, saying anything. I put up my hands like, I surrender, and followed them to the bathroom. I had clearly pissed her off again, though I have no idea when. She was getting me back for whatever it was I had done to her by doing the thing she knew I hated most. Vicky sat down on the edge of the tub and leaned forward for Grace to light the cigarette for her.

"I'll be the lookout," I said. "I'm really not into smoking." Vicky rolled her eyes at me, and I thought I might throw up. How could I get them to leave the bathroom if I did? That's what I was working on. That, and what had I done to Vicky?

"Okay," Grace said, and lit her own cigarette. I looked out the bathroom window toward the driveway when Vicky started coughing. Grace coughed a little, too, but tried to cover it up by hopping onto the counter.

"My mother smokes," I said. I opened the window to get some air.

"Yeah?" Grace said, blowing smoke out at the same time.

"You have to be more careful if your parents are addicts," I explained. "It means you're more susceptible. My dad is an alcoholic."

"Recovering alcoholic," Vicky said to Grace, as if I were exaggerating or something. "He hasn't had a drink in like ten years."

"Eleven," I said. "But still, it means I have to be that much more careful."

"My parents are both assholes. What does that say for me?" Vicky said. She and Grace cracked up, choking on the carcinogens in their lungs. I didn't think it was that funny.

"Watch out," Grace said, taking another drag. "Or you'll be an asshole, too!"

I was surprised, but Vicky laughed at that. I watched her sitting on the edge of the bathtub, bracing her hands on her knees. She looked totally unfamiliar to me. She seemed nasty, not happy, laughing that way. She shot me a look of such pure hatred, I didn't know what to do. I thought of apologizing, but that was stupid.

"Don't feel bad, though," Grace said. "My mother is Looney Tunes, so chances are I will be, too!" She wiped the little tears from the corners of her eyes and sniffed, still laughing.

Vicky laughed. "Loonier than my dad? He took off to find himself when I was ten, and now he works at Camp Snoopy in Florida."

"Loonier than that," Grace said. I wanted to tell them

to stop it, somebody's gonna lose an eye, somebody's gonna end up crying—the way Mom used to when Vicky and I were playing too rough. One time after Mom said that to us, Vicky pulled off Marya Beth's head. Usually it was me who ended up crying.

Grace took another drag. "My mom keeps all her stuff in the basement."

"Big deal," Vicky said. "I don't think that tops abandoning your wife and kids to spend your time dressed up in a dog suit singing about friendship."

"My mom keeps stuff in the basement, too," I said. Even as the words were coming out, I was telling myself, Shut up, shut up. Don't get involved or you end up holding the headless doll.

"I don't mean old sleeping bags," Grace said. She laughed again. "I mean *everything*. She moved down to the basement of our building because she thinks the TV told her to."

"Whoa," Vicky said. I sat down on the toilet seat.

"Yeah," Grace said. "She's manic-depressive, but she quit taking her drugs, you know, that keep her okay. She decided she didn't need them anymore. Isn't that brilliant? My dad wants to know when she went to med school. Now she's like, losing touch again."

I shook my head, and Vicky blew smoke up past her

hair. I guess they both got the smoking skill down, hurray hurray.

"So," Grace said. "Which makes me more receptible."

"Susceptible," I whispered, past the golf ball in my throat. Why don't I learn to keep my big mouth shut?

"Whatever. Wouldn't that be a great thing to inherit? And it is. Hereditary."

"Holy sh—," Vicky started saying.

The bathroom door flew open, and Mrs. Petowski stood there. Grace flipped her cigarette into the sink; Vicky held hers behind her back.

Little wisps of smoke were escaping from their noses.

"*What* are you *doing*?" Mrs. Petowski demanded. I had stopped looking out the window was why we got caught. Some lookout.

Vicky blew a long stream of smoke out of her mouth—there was a surprising amount still in there—and said, "We're smoking cigarettes."

Grace cracked up. Vicky looked at her, and for a second it was like they were best friends instead of enemies. Or maybe I'm overreacting. I was terrified. Caught ya red-handed—my nightmare fear.

Mrs. Petowski grabbed Vicky by the elbow and dragged her down the hall to her room. Vicky still had the cigarette in her hand. The door slammed, and all Grace and I could hear were muffled voices. Grace stubbed out her cigarette on the sink and then turned on the tap. "Get up," she said. I stood up and lifted the toilet lid so Grace could make a perfect shot from the counter. "Flush, stupid," she said.

The evidence, I thought, and pushed the handle. I closed the lid and sat back down. "What should we do?" I asked. Sitting in silence was killing me. I wanted to run, I wanted to get more details about Grace's mother, I wanted to apologize again for having called Grace crazy that time—everything. Should we stick around as moral support for Vicky, or should we get out?

"Let's go," Grace said.

The second we stepped into the hallway, Mrs. Petowski stuck her head out of Vicky's bedroom. "I'll be calling your mothers," she said. I nodded and looked at my feet. Grace put her hands on her hips.

"I'm sorry, Mrs. Petowski," I said. What a sap, what a brownnose. Why was I apologizing to her? But that's what I do when an adult is disappointed in me.

Grace turned and flew down the stairs. "Bye," I said stupidly, and followed Grace. I didn't let out my breath until we were outside, when I threw up all over Mrs. Petowski's dahlias.

fourteen

MOM AND DAD didn't say anything all through dinner, so I started thinking maybe Mrs. Petowski had really been bluffing. I dumped my food down the garbage disposal and went out back with my saxophone to practice not counting. Midway through "Moondance," Mom came out and sat next to me on the picnic table bench.

"Sounds good," she said.

I wiped off the mouthpiece. Spit is such disgusting stuff, although not until it gets outside your mouth, I guess.

"Something's bothering me," Mom said, leaning back with her elbows on the picnic table.

"What?"

"Mrs. Petowski called this afternoon at work. . . ."

"Mom, I'm so sorry, but listen—"

"Why didn't you tell me?"

"I don't know." Should I tell her I wasn't smoking?

"You could have told me you were smoking, Molly. Don't you feel like you can tell me things?"

Pang of guilt for not letting her know about my period. "Of course, Mom. I can tell you anything." Ha-ha. I can't even explain most of what I do to myself.

"Well, I realize that hiding in the bathroom with your friends to smoke is a way to act cool. . . ."

"I know, I know," I said. "Smoking is terrible for you and stupid and deadly and everything, and I've been lecturing you about it, so now you think I'm a total hypocrite, but. . ."

"Well, that's true, although that's not what gets me." Mom leaned forward and looked at me over my saxophone. "What bothers me is, if you wanted to try smoking, why didn't you ask me?"

"Ask you what?"

"If you want to smoke, Molly, you should come to me. I don't want you to sneak around behind my back."

"Mom, I wasn't sneaking. I wasn't even smoking."

"Molly, I'm not yelling at you. Please don't lie to me. That's what makes me crazy. Here." She pulled a pack of cigarettes out of her pocketbook, took out two, and handed one to me. "I would prefer that you never started, Molly, but it's worse to think you feel like you have to lie to me." She took out her lighter and held out the flame toward me.

"No, seriously, Mom." I held the cigarette away. "I wasn't smoking. I was being the lookout."

"The lookout?"

When she said it like that, it sounded so stupid and juvenile. I put down the cigarette on the picnic table. Then my hands felt really stupid and empty, like they needed something to do, so I took the mouthpiece off my saxophone and stuck it in its holder.

"Yeah, the lookout."

"While your friends were smoking?"

"Yeah," I said. "I hate smoke."

Mom sighed and picked up the cigarette from the picnic table. She wiggled it back into the pack, then lit her own and looked up at the sky.

"So you were the lookout?"

I laughed. "Don't say it like that."

"Like what?"

"The lookout? The lookout? You make me feel like a total reject."

"Oh, Molly," Mom said. We both started laughing.

"You're supposed to be happy I'm making wise choices

about my health, Mom."

"I am, I am," she said, and took another drag.

"But what?"

She laughed. "You're just so serious, Mol. You are so damned serious."

"And nice," I said.

"The nicest person I know."

I took the rest of my saxophone apart and put it away, then shut the case. I had practiced for only fifteen minutes, at most. "If you were in my grade, you'd be like Keiko. Even if deep down you liked me, you'd be friends with Alissa and Wendy and those girls, instead."

"Molly," Mom said, like, How could I say that, but also like, Yeah, that's true.

"Not that Keiko likes me anymore."

"I'm sure she does. You should give her a call."

"You'd be in the in crowd if you were my age. You're still in the in crowd, and you're a grown-up."

She stubbed out her cigarette on the table. "I just . . . are you okay, Molly? I worry about you."

"I'm okay," I said. I played with the latch of my saxophone case.

"Maybe you should call Keiko up right now, ask if she wants to help you serve at the dinner party Labor Day. That might be fun, huh? I'll give you each ten dollars.

And she can sleep over. It might be really fun! What do you say?"

I didn't feel like talking about that. Why couldn't she remember what it was like to be fourteen? You don't just call up somebody who's popular if you're not and say, Hey, wanna sleep over? I had to change the subject; Mom was getting all psyched about her idea. "Remember the time Vicky pulled the head off my doll?"

"Yeah, Marya Beth," Mom said. She folded one leg under her and sat on it. I knew that would distract her. She always liked Marya Beth, I think because her parents gave me that doll the day I was born. Mom had dreamed while she was in labor that she was having twins—Molly Beth and Marya Beth. "Phew, you were like shell-shocked, standing there holding headless Marya Beth out at me." She imitated me, big-eyed and frowning, and I laughed. She's so cute and un-awkward; never even needed her teeth straightened. I ran my tongue along the inside of my lower lip, all cut up and slightly bloody from playing sax with bottom braces.

"It was pretty upsetting," I said.

"And Vicky had Marya Beth's head inside the little T-shirt that was yours when you were a baby, the pink one with the lace, right? God, that was weird, like she was possessed or something. I can't believe she just yanked Marya

125

Beth's head off. She was so rough for such a little person."

"She's still pretty rough," I said, and my stomach rumbled. "Sometimes I feel like if I'm not careful, she'll rip off *my* head."

"She freaked me out, dumping Marya Beth's head on the floor like that, thump, onto the kitchen floor."

"She dumped the head?"

"Oh, yeah. It was like something out of a horror movie. Hey, didn't Daddy and I sew the head back on?"

"Yeah," I said. "You made me and Vicky wait in the living room during the operation. Turned out crooked, though."

"What did?"

"The head." I sat straight on the bench and twisted my head toward Mom. "Like this."

"Really? You never said anything."

"Yeah. After that, any time I picked her up, she sort of looked at me out the corner of her eyes like, See what happened to me because of you."

"Oh, Molly," Mom said. "You are so damned hard on yourself!"

"I know." I stood my saxophone case on its side and tipped it toward me. "I hate that. It's one of my worst traits."

"Beat yourself up about it, why don't you?" She gave

me a little shove, and I smiled to show that I got it. "What made you think about Marya Beth?"

I shrugged and looked up at the sky. "Hey, that's Jupiter." I pointed and she glanced up. "You can tell it's a planet because planets don't twinkle."

"Really," she said. She checked her watch. Her show was about to start, so I could tell she wanted to tie things up with me and get inside. "Sorry about sewing her head on crooked."

"That's okay," I said. "You warned us not to play so rough."

"Well, good to know I did something right." She grabbed her pocketbook and stood up. "Guess I'll see what Daddy's doing."

"Okay," I said. I got my period, I said silently to her back as she walked in the house. I've been shoplifting. I read a really good book. I've been thinking about how death is going to feel. I like Jason, but he likes Grace. Vicky is destroying me. I'm out of control. "Be in in a minute," I said.

"Okay," Mom said at the door. She was letting bugs in, which would drive Dad nuts, but she didn't seem to care. "Good for you, resisting peer pressure and all that."

"Thanks," I said. I put my head down on my saxophone case and cried my eyes out.

fifteen

AFTER I COULDN'T cry anymore, I went in and sat on the stairs and watched my parents watching the Monday Crappy Movie. They love made-for-television movies, especially when there's a kidnapping or a wrongly accused mother or a psycho girlfriend. Mom had her feet right up on the couch, and her head was on Dad's lap. His arm was resting across her chest. The only time they talked was to say stuff like "You *idiot*!" to the guy in the movie. When will I find someone to be together with like that?

During a commercial, Mom looked up and saw me on the stairs and said I should come watch the movie with them. "I gotta call Vicky," I said, and went up to their bedroom.

I sprawled out on their huge bed and stared at the ceiling. No cracks. I was thinking about not calling Vicky. Ever again. Maybe it would be better if I just stopped being friends with her. Let her be with Grace, if that's what she wants, and they can smoke themselves to death for all I care. Grace is going back to her real life at the end of the month; Vicky better realize the only person she has here is me. Not that I have any back-up friends, either. And maybe Grace will help Vicky get in with the popular girls. Then I'd be completely alone. I'm trapped. I wish I had skipped first grade when I had the chance, and not been so scared of the older kids. When will I find a group to be in? Too bad I'm not ethnic or black like the girl in *The Bluest Eye*; maybe that would be an easier way to have an identity.

The bookmark Nadine had left in *Beloved* when she lent it to me was a piece of pink paper with her name and phone number. Maybe she needs a friend, too. Oh, that's likely. I'm so sure she wants a fourteen-year-old loser for a friend. She seems like she has enough friends, anyway. Probably she could tell how lonely I am and was just being nice, or was wishing for somebody to talk with about the book. I should finish reading *Beloved* before I call her, so I have something to say. . . . I dialed her number—which I have memorized—and when somebody answered, a woman, maybe her, I hung up. Then I dialed Keiko's number but hung up before it even rang.

I pressed #5 for Vicky, automatic dial, and she picked up right away. When she heard it was me, she started whispering. "Are you grounded?"

"No," I whispered back. "Are you?"

"Sort of."

"What does that mean?"

"Can you come over tomorrow?"

"Yeah."

"Good. About three. I'm not supposed to be on the phone."

"Did you call Grace?"

"No. Maybe just you could come over. We have to talk."

"What happened?"

"Coming!" she yelled. "I'm dead. Gotta go. Three o'clock?"

"Okay."

She hung up. I held the phone for a while and then dialed Grace. She said Mrs. Petowski had left a message for her mother, but Grace erased it, so she wasn't in any trouble at all. She told me I was lucky to have such cool parents. I guess, I said.

"It's gonna rain tomorrow," she said. "You want to go

to the arcade after you're done at The Nail Place?"

"Um," I answered. "Well, Vicky was grounded, so I was thinking maybe I'd go over there for a while."

"Oh, okay. That sounds good."

"Actually she sounded pretty upset," I lied. Maybe. It's hard to tell when Vicky is upset, really. "I think maybe, I don't know . . ."

"Vicky doesn't want me to come."

"It's not that. It's just . . ."

"That's okay, that's cool," Grace said. "I should hang out some with Simone, anyway. Call me tomorrow night, okay?"

"Okay," I said.

I'm lying on my bed now, writing all this down and trying to figure out what's missing again. I feel so empty, so disgusted with myself for being psyched that Vicky and Grace both still like me best. My room looks totally foreign to me. Is this my room? Or did I take a wrong turn and end up in somebody else's room, somebody else's life? Maybe my life is out there going on happily without me in it.

Or is this who I really am? I don't feel like doing anything, even reading. Everything used to be so clear to me—what I believed in, like be loyal, be good; what I was against, like smoking and stealing and being lazy; even who I was, either a beautiful little princess or a tortured genius who would someday grow up to be president. Now I feel like I don't know anything. I think maybe I'm everything I hate and have no respect for. Maybe I'm nasty and petty, and my only ambition is to be liked.

Maybe I'm nobody.

sixteen

VICKY CRACKED AN egg on my head and rubbed it in. "She said that? She really said you should've smoked?"

"Not in so many words, but yeah," I said. "Are you sure you read the instructions right? This smells gross."

"I read it, I read it. Look, it's right here." She shoved the *Cosmo* over to me with her foot. When I looked down to read the article, a glop of egg plopped down on the page.

"Molly, trust me." She pulled the magazine back. Vicky has more supplies than anybody I know. She always likes to have a project going in her room, with her desk chair nudged under her doorknob and every supply we can think of all on top of newspapers laid out on her rug.

"Here, now wrap the Saran Wrap around your head."

"Okay." I pulled a long sheet off the roll, and it all stuck to itself. I sliced my finger on the little metal cutting edge. "Damn," I said, and put my finger in my mouth.

"Hurry, or you won't get all the conditioning benefits." Vicky cracked an egg over her own head and massaged vigorously. I finally got the piece of Saran Wrap off the roll, but it was hard to straighten out because my cut was still bleeding and I had to keep sucking my finger.

"Hurry! I need some!"

"Okay, okay," I said. "I'm hurrying. But I'm also bleeding."

"Let me see."

I showed her my finger and squeezed it so she could see the blood coming out.

"Oh, please."

"Seriously." I bopped her over her soggy head with the box of Saran Wrap, using my unwounded left hand. "I'm hemorrhaging. I'm getting dizzy from blood loss."

She tore off a perfect piece of Saran Wrap and wound it like a turban on her eggy hair. "Wait till you see how shiny our hair is," she said. "Pass me the Nutter Butters."

I handed her the bag and she took out two, one for each of us.

"That's really weird, Molly. I can't believe your mother said that."

"Yeah," I said. I opened up the Nutter Butter and scraped off the filling with my bottom teeth. I like to eat the filling first, then the cookie part. Maybe Nadine would be interested, I was thinking. "What did your mother end up doing?"

"Well, she calmed down eventually." Vicky took another cookie and ate it in two bites. "Basically she doesn't want me hanging around with Grace anymore."

"Really?"

"Really." She ate another Nutter Butter. "Bad influence. You know."

"Wow," I said. "You must be so pissed."

"I don't know," Vicky said, adjusting her turban and checking her watch. "Ten more minutes. There's egg running down your neck."

"Ew!" I pulled a handful of paper towels off the roll and swabbed up my neck. Nothing was leaking out of Vicky's. She was eating another Nutter Butter. Once Vicky gets going, there's no stopping her. She can outeat my father. One time last year after she got in a big fight with Alissa, she polished off a gallon of Heavenly Hash ice cream, a box of Fig Newtons, two and a half pieces of pizza, and four bowls of Raisin Bran. Then she didn't eat anything the whole next week except one piece of Brannola toast a day, no butter or anything.

"For how long?" I asked.

"How long what?"

"Are you not supposed to hang around with Grace?"

"Oh," she said. "Ever."

"Ever? Come on . . ."

"Ever. And in a way, she's right."

"Vicky, that's ridiculous. It's not Grace's fault. She didn't influence us."

"We have to talk, Molly."

I held out my Blistex to her, and she took it, I think without even noticing. Egg was oozing down my neck again; it felt like brain.

"We never stole before," she said.

I took another Nutter Butter and unscrewed it, then screwed it back together and put it down on the newspaper. "One mascara."

"And a pack of Life Savers. And you never told me. How do you think I felt? She assumed I knew, of course. Why wouldn't I? I'm your best friend . . . ."

"Is the time up yet? This is really gross."

"Six more minutes," Vicky said. "I can't believe you stole."

I moved the Blistex tube across the newspaper, watching

it like it was a little kid's toy car. "Did you tell your mother?"

"No! I wouldn't do that to you, Mol. Come on. I mean, I wouldn't tell my mother on Alissa Barton. But maybe she has a point, you know?"

"Grace didn't make me do it." Why was I defending Grace? I had specifically asked her not to tell Vicky. Obviously she was so desperate for Vicky to like her that she sold me out.

"Well, duh," Vicky said.

I rolled my eyes and pulled over the *Cosmo* to see how strict you really have to be about the time. I hate when people say *well, duh*.

"I wasn't saying she held a gun to your head, Mol. I'm just saying you haven't really been acting like yourself since that day in the arcade."

"What day in the arcade? Last week?"

"No, that first day. You know, when she came over and played Bop the Badger against you. I would never go up to a complete stranger and play Bop the Badger on her quarter, would you? She's like—she's the type who always barges through the front door of a party. We're more like, slowly blend in through the side, you know?"

"I guess," I said.

She ate another cookie. "Well, and it's having an effect

on both of us. Something is different, don't you think?"

"I don't know." I wiped my neck with more paper towels. Vicky's was still fine.

"I mean, like you didn't used to act so sluttish around Henry, and . . ."

"What do you mean?"

She checked her watch. "One more minute." She stood up and yanked the chair away from the door. "Come on, let's go."

I followed her to the bathroom. "What do you mean, sluttish?"

"Nothing, it's just . . . Here, hold your head under the faucet." She ran the water over her fingers to check the temperature and nodded. I stuck my head under the tap. She kept talking, but I couldn't hear her. She massaged my head while the water ran over it. My eyes were clamped shut at first to keep the egg from running into them, but after a minute I relaxed, as much as it is possible to relax bent over a bathroom sink. It felt great having my head massaged like that. It's my favorite part of getting a haircut—when Janine at the beauty parlor massages my head. Vicky was just about as good as Janine, and Janine is a pro.

"There," Vicky said after a few minutes. She turned off the water and squeezed out my hair, then put a towel over it and wrapped it. "My turn." She stuck her head under the faucet. I thought I should massage her head, but she did it herself, instead.

When she finished rinsing and wrapped a towel around her hair, I asked, "What do you mean, I act sluttish?"

"Shh." She walked down the hall to her room, and I followed her. After she wedged the chair back under the doorknob, she took the towel off her head and sat down to comb out her hair. "Ow," she said. "Is yours all knotty?"

"Yeah," I said, trying to pull her big tortoiseshell comb through my hair. "I talked to him once on the beach. I'm sorry, I really don't think that's so sluttish."

"I saw how you were looking at him at my birthday dinner. Anyway, it's not that, Molly." She grabbed two Nutter Butters and ate them at the same time. "I know you don't even realize it, but I think you're sort of imitating Grace. Even that thing she does with her hair, you know?" She pushed her bangs back with her pinkie and thumb. I blushed.

"So? My bangs are growing out."

"That's not the point. I think you're losing yourself. You're being like . . . like Grace, and I just think . . ."

"What?"

"You do whatever you want. I just know I'm not allowed to hang out with her."

I concentrated on combing, trying to avoid the spot Vicky had wounded two nights earlier, because it was still pretty tender.

"You've got some thinking to do, Molly, that's all. I mean, you say you're my best friend. If that's true, well, maybe lately it seems like if it came down to it, you wouldn't choose me."

"Vicky, that's not true."

"I just know I'd stand by you, no matter what. And Grace, well, like, she was like, 'Don't tell Molly I told you, but . . .'"

"Really?"

"You're my best friend, Molly. I just thought you should know. She's not someone you can trust. But you have to make your own decisions."

She took the comb from me and started working very gently on my tangles, holding on to the roots so it wouldn't hurt as much. I closed my eyes and tried to take a rest from thinking.

seventeen

"SO WHAT DID you and Vicky do yesterday?" Grace called me at about eight o'clock this morning, and Mom had to wake me up for Grace to ask me that.

"Um, nothing," I said, trying to collect myself. Mom was in her bathroom putting on makeup while I talked on her phone.

"Is she really grounded? Her mother is such a witch!"

"She's not that bad." I was annoyed at her for saying that about Mrs. Petowski. What did Grace know about her? Left alone with two kids and no money, anybody might start being a little sharp around the edges. But I guess mostly I was just mad at Grace for telling Vicky about scungilli.

"Oh," Grace said. "So anyway, you want me to meet you at The Nail Place later? We can walk down to volleyball together."

"Is it Wednesday already?"

"Yeah. Did I wake you up?"

"No, but um . . ." I tried to come up with an excuse. I just didn't feel like hanging out with her. "Well, I have my saxophone lesson, so . . ."

"That's at eight tonight, right?"

"Yeah, but I really have to practice."

"All afternoon?"

"And also, I'm not feeling that well. I mean, I might just go home, after."

"Oh," she said. Pretty lame excuse. "I hope you feel better."

"Thanks," I said.

"Call me later."

"Okay." I waited for her to hang up. I always do that in case at the last second before hanging up, the other person says something that I wouldn't want to miss. I would've confronted her about betraying my trust, but how could I, with Mom standing right there in the bathroom, eavesdropping? Although maybe Mom is the only one who'd be impressed that I shoplifted. No, but she'd be happy if I told her, probably; if I confided in her. I guess it was more that I hate confrontations. I figured Grace was leaving August 25 anyway, two weeks from tomorrow. Why get into avoidable hassles?

Mom came out of the bathroom brushing her hair and sat on the bed next to me. "What was that?"

"Nothing," I said.

"Trouble with Grace?"

"She's just . . . I don't know. Nothing."

"So what was that whole story, 'have my saxophone lesson.' What was that all about?" She shook my foot and smiled at me. I pulled my foot away. I wasn't in the mood for her cutesiness.

"Nothing. Okay? Nothing."

"Okay," she said. She stood up and disappeared into the bathroom again. I pulled her pillow over my head and thought about suffocating myself but instead threw it back on the bed, got up, and went down to stare into the refrigerator for a while.

"You want a ride?" Mom reached around me to get the orange juice. I couldn't look at her, I felt so guilty for being nasty before.

"No, I'll run."

"You're looking really skinny," she said.

"Thanks."

"Maybe too skinny. You're getting dark circles under

your eyes, and you sound like you're losing your voice. Want some milk and an English muffin with cottage cheese? I bought you whole milk instead of skim. . . ."

"I'm fine." I went upstairs and got into my running clothes. She's so nice to me. No wonder everybody likes her. When I was nasty, she distanced herself from the situation instead of yelling at me or trying to work it out. I would definitely, in the same position—for instance, with Vicky—try to work it out and end up with less hair.

I made it to The Nail Place in sixteen minutes, my best time ever. I kept saying to myself, Faster, faster. I wished I could keep going for an hour. The wind lifted my hair, and the ground pushed back against my feet. I felt powerful, like if someone were after me, I could get away, I could save myself. Maybe Nadine was wrong; maybe I have a survival instinct like the lady in the hospital. But is there anything I could focus my being proud on? I don't even have pierced ears.

Every time Mom smiled at me all morning, I looked down at the counter. I felt so guilty. It was too late to tell her I'd gotten my period: my period was already over. Maybe next time I get it, I'll tell her it's my first time, and the real first time will be all my own. And Vicky's and Grace's, of course.

Vicky stopped by at one to see if I wanted to walk

down to volleyball with her. I took her in the back where Soraya does the waxing (Why would women allow hot wax to be poured on their sensitive areas and ripped off? It seems a bit extreme to me.) and told her about my phone conversation with Grace this morning.

She loved it. She seemed happier than I'd seen her all summer. I guess it's been hard on Vicky, like I was pulling away from her, and I know how terrified she is of that. I mean, I was a wreck when I thought she was ditching me for Grace. And Vicky has a much bigger fear of abandonment than I do.

I told her that at first I tried to use saxophone as an excuse, until Grace said isn't that at eight? "No way! Oh, that's so embarrassing," Vicky whispered. We both had our hands over our mouths to keep from bursting out laughing. Vicky was rocking back and forth. "So what did you say?"

"I have to *practice*!"

That was it. She laughed so hard, tears were running down her face. "Practice? All afternoon?"

"That's what *she* said!"

We were cracking up uncontrollably. She had to run out of the waxing room and into the bathroom. I went in, too. She doesn't mind, if it's me.

When we finally calmed down, she said, "So I guess

we're not going to the volleyball game!" We cracked up all over again. Mom came back to get a new bag of cotton balls and smiled at us. She never yells about laughing too loud like Vicky's mother sometimes does; Mom always looks relieved when I laugh.

"You wanna go over to the arcade?"

"I guess," I said. I don't love the arcade, but what else were we going to do? There's not that much to do here. Kids from off-island mostly go to camp. And besides, I was wearing just a T-shirt and my sports bra, no sweatshirt. Ten pounds down, five to go, and I could really feel the difference. Maybe some summer people, some cute guys, would be at the arcade, and they would see me fresh and think I was okay-looking and want to come up and introduce themselves, and we could have a summer romance and then become pen pals.

When we got to the arcade, there were two ten-year-old boys playing Super Kamikaze Warriors and that's it. We got change from the machine and Vicky tried the driving game. I watched. At least it was cool in there.

I was playing Bop the Badger when Grace walked in with Simone. It was like total deja vu. I tried pretending I didn't see her, but it was too late; she spotted me as soon as she walked in, and headed right toward me. I kept bopping badgers, waiting for her to bawl me out—why did I lie, all that. Should I counter-confront her? Why did *you* lie?

Instead of saying anything, she picked up the other bopper, just like back in July when I first met her, and bopped away with me. We didn't say anything. When the game ended, we got the bonus. I smiled at her, because without her help I wouldn't have gotten into the bonus. She didn't look up, as if she had to concentrate so hard for when the badgers started popping up again. After the bonus round, she turned away, grabbed Simone by the shoulders, and left the arcade. Simone looked back at me as she was being pushed out the door.

eighteen

"ARE YOU SICK again?" Henry asked.

"No," I said. I was putting my saxophone together and feeling really nervous because I hadn't practiced nearly enough. We were down in the Petowskis' basement where I have my lesson, and Vicky was waiting up in her room for me. She had spent the rest of the afternoon reassuring me that I did the right thing by not saying anything to Grace at the arcade. She thought Grace had made a fool of herself, coming up to us. The more Vicky tried to convince me of how well I'd handled things, though, the less sure I felt.

"You sound pretty hoarse," Henry said. "Too much partying lately?"

I smiled without showing my braces. As if. Yeah, I

148

have so many parties to go to.

"Practice much?"

"Not that much," I said.

"How come?" He leaned back on the green vinyl couch and spread his arms over the back.

"How come?"

"Yeah. I mean, you're not lazy. You don't seem like the type to just blow it off—are you?"

"No." My voice was hardly coming out. I cleared my throat but did it the abrasive way, out of habit. It was getting pretty raw-feeling. "No," I said again. It sounded very raspy, and I wondered if Henry found it sexy. Probably not.

"What, then? Is it because of your braces?"

"No." I didn't like it that he noticed my braces, although, honestly, you can't miss them. "I don't like how I sound."

"Do you remember that time you and Vicky decided to teach yourselves to do cartwheels? I was baby-sitting for you guys?"

"Yeah. I couldn't do it, surprise surprise."

"But remember what you did? I'll never forget it. Vicky went up to her room to paint or something, and you stayed out there in the backyard flipping over, slamming onto your back."

I put my head down in my hands. "I didn't know anybody was *watching*."

"No, it was great," Henry said. I looked up at him, and he was leaning forward toward me. "That's how I think I'll always picture you."

"As a seven-year-old doing uncoordinated cartwheels," I said. "Great."

"No, seriously. That's why I said I'd teach you saxophone this summer. You were the coolest little kid, so determined, so, I don't know, strong."

I licked the reed and started right in on "Moondance" because I really didn't want to talk about it anymore. I stopped immediately, though, because the first note was so loud I think Henry jumped. "Sorry," I said.

"That's okay. Keep going."

I took a breath and started again, but it's tough to play the saxophone quietly. That's why if I ever practice, I do it outside. I don't want to blast people away.

I got through the whole first section without a mistake, but as soon as I realized that, I messed up on the next note and stopped.

"Sorry."

"That's okay."

"Start from the beginning?"

"No, keep going."

I backed up two measures and started over, and made it slowly through the whole song without any more mistakes. It's not that huge an accomplishment; I've been working on "Moondance" since February.

"Okay," Henry said, but not until after I looked up at him. "You're still counting the pauses, huh?"

"I don't get it." I unhooked the sax from my neck holder. "If I don't count out the rhythm, I'll get it wrong."

"No, you won't."

"Trust me."

"And don't be afraid to be loud," he said. "Let's hear it again."

I played it a few times through. When the half hour was up, I think he was relieved. I guess I've improved a little this summer; I make fewer mistakes in the songs I need to do for band, but I can't help feeling that Henry is deeply disappointed in me. I hate that. I hate disappointing anybody. The more I try to get it, though, the more I try not to count and not to make mistakes, the more I screw up.

"Do the last section again one more time," Henry said. "And maybe, I don't know, try to make it sound like you're not hating it."

I smiled with the mouthpiece between my teeth and started over. When I got through, Nadine was on the stairs, looking at me under the banister and clapping. Henry turned around to face her. We hadn't heard her come down.

"That sounded good," she said.

"Not really," I mumbled. I don't like playing a solo in front of anybody. Henry is different, a little; at least my mother pays him to listen to me squawk.

"Nadine," Henry said, "we're in the middle of a lesson."

"I'll be quiet." She moved to the back of the step she was sitting on. Henry let out a loud breath and turned to me.

"That was a little better," he said. "But it still sounds . . . tense."

"Sorry."

"You have to stop counting out the beats!" He rubbed his palms together. It was pretty clear he was nervous with Nadine there. "You know what I mean?"

"Yes," I said. I wanted to make him look good in front of her.

"I don't know what you mean," Nadine said.

"Nadine!" He glared over his shoulder at her.

"What? I don't. Molly, do you really understand that?"

"Well, sort of," I said. My rules of allegiance were feeling a little screwed up.

"What I mean is," Henry said to Nadine, "she counts. She goes like one, two, three, four, and each note is a total panic, instead of a part of a phrase!" He was so exasperated, he was yelling.

"Okay, that sort of makes sense to me," Nadine said. She moved up to the front of the step again. "So play the whole song, and screw it if you mess up. Right?"

"Exactly," Henry said. They both looked at me, and Henry asked, "Does that make sense?"

"Sure," I said. I couldn't tell if they were in a fight or not. I took my saxophone apart and put it away as fast as possible so I could get out. I thanked Henry while I was latching the case, and started up the stairs.

As I passed Nadine, she stood up and said, "I used to panic that I'd make a mistake, too."

"Really?"

"Yeah. Then I decided, so what?"

"Um," I said, leaning against the wall and banging the saxophone case against my legs. "I've been wondering. You know that lady with the chest wound and the earrings?"

"Yeah."

"Did she die?"

"Yeah," Nadine said. "But first she lived. Hey, Henry, we should get going."

As I lugged my saxophone to Vicky's room, I was imagining what it would be like to go out on the sailboat with Nadine and Henry. Maybe Henry would ask me to fix the telltales on the jib so he could judge the wind better, and I'd say, "Sure!" I'd be very agile and unafraid walking on the deck, and I'd fix the telltales with no problem.

Then I'd stand up there on the bow of the boat with the wind blowing over my tan body, which would be in the white bikini that still has the tags on it in my drawer, and I would know that Henry was in the stern thinking I was a sexy young woman. Not a bumbling, awkward girl; a strong, sexy young woman. Is that terrible to wish for? Is that subjugating me to bimbo sex-symbol status? I like the idea of it, even if I shouldn't: feeling like maybe I could be a sexy, sensual person.

Nadine and Henry would be thinking, Wow, she's terrific, so alive and smart and sexy and fun to be with; and the sun would be setting right ahead of us while I stood up in the bow, holding on to the forestay and balancing perfectly in the wind.

nineteen

I'M SO MAD I can't even write today.

twenty

I HATE HER.

Who's going to be the best woman at my wedding?

What if nobody ever cares about me?

Am I overreacting?

I have to tape up all these torn pages. Which means I literally have to sort through my life from my birthday on and piece it back together. Maybe I should just leave it and throw all the pages in the garbage where they belong.

No, I promised myself I'd be able to read this when I'm old, when I've cute-ified everything that happened, when I'm looking back on all this stuff and laughing. The sight of fourteen pounds of Scotch tape on the pages should stop that and make me remember.

Start from the beginning, if I can find it. Start from where I think I left off.

Blah, blah, blah, ate dinner, had my saxophone lesson (oops, I think I wrote about that), broke a nail, slept, jogged, worked, saw Jason walking down Leeward Street with my former friend Grace, ate a doughnut, threw it up. Vicky came by The Nail Place after Soraya did a wrap on the pinkie nail that I broke last night. It had seemed like a big deal for a second because it was my longest nail and I thought of it as being the most delicate, feminine part of me. Then after my lesson, Vicky had this great idea that we should try dive rolls on her bed, which was fun until I slammed my hand into her wall, which cracked the glass on the clown picture she had hanging there, and also broke my nail. To her credit, Vicky was more concerned that I had hurt myself than about her picture, which her father bought her in Montreal back when he was sane, as Vicky puts it. Although after I left, she was probably pissed about the painting. No, now I'm just being nasty.

But anyway, I managed not to yank off the split nail, even though it was very tempting. I kept touching it where it was split, but I used my self-control like Mom said I should, and resisted. Mom put a Band-Aid around it and even called Soraya at home to make a special appointment for 10:00 A.M., and then Mom and I sat on the porch and drank raspberry tea. It was a good night until I got into bed and started worrying that Vicky was mad at me for cracking the glass, and that maybe I hadn't apologized enough. Then I started stressing that maybe I'm still fat, or on the other hand, that all this feeling like I'm in control of one thing, of my body, at least, is a total illusion, when really maybe I'm getting crazy obsessive about body size. I was such a nervous wreck that I couldn't sleep, so I just stared at the crack in my ceiling and felt my ribs until it was light out. When I was brushing my teeth, it occurred to me that if I were in a Duracell battery commercial right then, I'd be the toy using the brand without the copper tops.

So my pinkie nail was fixed and actually looks better now than it did before, and feels stronger. Maybe that's an omen, as Grace would say if she were talking to me, which she's not.

I called Vicky before I jogged to work, and I was right: she was angry at me, but she wouldn't say why. I apologized some more about the glass and asked her please to stop by The Nail Place so we could do something fun, just the two of us.

She came by around two, and we walked all the way back to my house because it was overcast and she didn't feel like going to the arcade or the beach. As we walked, we kicked a pebble back and forth between us and talked about high school. I promised her again that I wouldn't switch into honors math and leave her alone in regular. She needs my help. It felt good to be so needed, I have to admit, even if it means I'll definitely never be an engineer. I wouldn't want to be an engineer, anyway.

On the way, she asked which I would choose to be if I had the choice: incredibly beautiful or incredibly brilliant. She said she would choose beautiful, because life is so much easier for a beautiful person. I said yeah, but life is so much more interesting for a brilliant person. She thought I was kidding.

We were the only ones home, so we went up to my room and put on the ceiling fan and lay head to toe on my bed cooling off. She told me what new school clothes she's going to get, maybe some dresses this year. She wants to have a more innocent look. I was spacing out a little. I figure my look will be jeans and sweatshirts again, leave it at that.

Then she was talking about how Freddy was looking at her so much at volleyball last Sunday, and did she look fat? No. Maybe she should try to like Freddy, she said. She's liked Freddy for over a year, but when I told her last February that I thought she had a crush on him, she didn't talk to me for a week, so I just said, "Maybe you should."

"Do you think you would want to go out with Jason again? We could double-date, maybe all walk down to the arcade together after school," she said.

"I think he's going out with Grace." I twirled a piece of my hair into a tight twist and cleared my throat. I had almost total laryngitis.

"Uck. Don't even say her name to me. Wasn't I right about her?"

"I guess," I think I said.

"Besides, she's leaving in two weeks, and then he's all yours."

"As if," I said. "Anyway, I never liked him that much in the first place."

"You did so!"

"No. I just went out with him because he's the first person who ever asked me. No big deal."

"Come on, you were into him. You were a wreck when he dumped you."

"I was not," I said. I got up on my elbows and looked at her. She was on her side, with my teddy bear wedged under her arm as a support.

"Oh, please. Your Prince Purple Flower. 'He's *such* a good kisser,'" Vicky said, imitating me. "Making out behind your dad's toolshed. Come on."

"I never said that."

"You've gotta be kidding! I remember you saying that on the phone: 'He's *such* a good kisser.' At least don't lie. You were totally infatuated, following him around like a lost puppy."

That's what she used to call me when I was going out with him; she was always saying I looked like a lost puppy, just because I sometimes went by his locker between classes. So what? It really pissed me off when she called me that. Did I look that desperate? Could I help it? It was so exciting to me to be going out with him, maybe I did make a fool of myself. But so what? That's ancient history now. Over and done. He's out of my life. I almost said shut up to her, but I stopped myself. "I was not," I said instead.

She didn't say anything and neither did I. How embarrassing, I was thinking. I never should have told her that we made out behind the toolshed that day, that he rubbed my neck when we were kissing after he found me back there when I ran after the tennis ball we'd been playing catch with. How he ran his thumb up the front of my neck while we were kissing and it made me feel so vulnerable and turned on. Why did I tell anybody that? I remember, though; I was so pumped after, I ran right in and called Vicky and told her every detail. She kept saying uh-huh, uh-huh, and I thought she was really happy for me, but it turns out she thought I was a slut. I didn't have sex with him, I said. We just kissed. I paid attention in sex ed. I know the high rate of teenage pregnancy; I know about increased chances of cervical cancer and AIDS if you have sex young or with multiple partners—we were just making out! What's wrong with that? Plenty, she said, and hung up on me.

I never should've told her. And about Prince Purple Flower. How embarrassing! Why had I ever told her I imagined Jason as Prince Purple Flower coming to rescue me from my boring life and ride off into the sunset to live happily ever after? And when?

"What about Prince Purple Flower?" My voice was almost nonexistent.

"You're the one who said it, not me." She was staring at my ceiling. "You know, they didn't fix the crack when they painted your ceiling. Doesn't that bug you?"

"No," I said. "What did I say about Prince Purple Flower?"

"I don't know."

"When did I tell you about that?"

"How should I remember? What's the difference? The point is, you liked him a lot, and you still like him."

"I never told you about Prince Purple Flower." I sat up. "I never told anybody about Prince Purple Flower."

"What do you think, I have ESP?"

"I think you read my journal." I was shaking. My hands were holding on to each other between my knees. It was so obvious. My brain was all over the place. What else could she have read? What had I written about her that would make her upset, I crazily thought. All that embarrassing stuff about being so lonely, about enchanted places and wishing I could take a break and scungilli. Oh.

Vicky was lying on her back on my bed, with her arms over her face, not moving a muscle. I picked up the journal off my night table and flipped through the pages covered in my scrawl, big some places and little in others, with the doodles around the dates and the smudges where I had to get the schmutz off the pen.

"That's how you found out about the Life Savers, isn't it? And the mascara."

She still didn't say anything, which I took as agreement.

"You read my journal," I said, closing it.

She sat up and dropped my teddy bear on the floor. "So what? Don't make a soap opera out of it. You think your life is so fascinating and private?"

She got off my bed and grabbed the journal from me.

"You think this is such special stuff? You know what? I was bored when I read it."

You shouldn't have read it, I tried to say, but my voice was gone and I was crying.

She opened up the journal and started reading in a voice like the one my father uses when he reads aloud the corniest Hallmark cards: *Wishing you joy on this special day/That never, ever goes away.* But she was reading my life like that, in this horrible, high, la-di-da voice: "'*Something's missing. I just spent five minutes staring into the refrigerator, but it wasn't in there. . . .*'" It sounded so stupid, so juvenile and self-indulgent and ridiculous in her mocking voice. My most private thoughts. This is what rape must feel like.

I grabbed the journal from her, or tried. It turned into a tug-of-war, and somehow paper started to rip. I wish I could say that *she* did it, that she stood there and tore it in front of me while I was maybe tied up or something, but that's not what happened. I let her tear it. I helped her tear it. I'm so ashamed. I can't even really remember what happened, just the sound, that twitchy *sh-sh-sh* of the textured paper ripping. Not just paper, pages: my words on them turned them into pages.

When it was done, there were shreds all over my rug. Vicky sat down on my bed, the burgundy and gray-marbled cover still clutched in her fist. I sat next to her and held my head in my hands like if I let go, it might explode. She pulled her Blistex from her fanny pack and held it out to me. I watched it dangle in front of me and didn't take it.

I took a deep breath, and suddenly I was calm. The buzzing in my head stopped. Isn't that weird? Not taking the Blistex, realizing I *could* not take it, had this totally calming effect. I don't have to take her damned Blistex.

I walked over to the closet and moved Marya Beth to the side so I could take my tape recorder out of the shoe box. I put in a fresh tape and turned it on.

"Get out," I said. It was barely audible, so I tried again, whispering, "Get out." Part of me couldn't believe I was saying that. It wasn't nice. A good host doesn't tell her guest to get out.

She started crying and sank down on the floor. "I'm sorry, Molly. I'm so sorry. Can you ever forgive me?"

"No," I whispered. It was true, and the truth coming out like that—so hard and not nice—felt, I'm a little embarrassed to say, exhilarating. I couldn't look at her, so I leaned against the wall, right where Prince Purple Flower used to be. The thought occurred to me that maybe I was making this all up; maybe this whole thing was some elaborate fantasy as unreal as when I used to imagine slaying dragons and marrying Prince Purple Flower and becoming president of the United States.

"I feel so guilty," Vicky said. "What can I do? How can I make it up to you? Here, I'll fix it. I'll fix it. I'll tape it back together." She flattened a crumpled piece and rotated it on the floor so the writing faced her.

"I want you to leave," I said as loudly as I could. Why am I not crying? I was thinking, but I didn't feel like crying. Things felt absolutely nonemotional. I had to get her out. That was the only objective in my life.

"Fine," she said, and stood up. "If you want me to go, I'm gone. But you just lost the best friend you ever had. Don't think you can crawl back and apologize this time. Now you've proven what kind of person you are, and I promise: every day of high school will be hell for you."

I believed her, but I didn't reconsider. I knew she was hurting; I knew I was hurting her and that she would do everything possible to get revenge. But honestly, how much more hellish could it get? "Good-bye, Vicky."

She stomped across my room and tried to slam my door shut, but my carpeting is so thick that it's hard to do. She managed with the front door, though. I turned off the tape recorder and stood there alone in the middle of my shredded life, thinking, Where do I go from here?

twenty-one

DEAR FUTURE ME, reading this.

Did you find this journal under a pile of old pajamas while you were packing up the room to go off to college or your own apartment? Do you remember me? The gawky teenager who spent the last couple of weeks of the summer before high school taping the ripped-up pieces of this journal back together? Are you (am I?) still the same?

Just a few things I want you to know, me.

It hurts. It really hurts to be me right now, sometimes. I don't know if any decisions I'm making are good ones, smart ones, or even important ones. They all sure as hell feel earth-shattering. For instance, I decided to switch into honors math. Who knows, maybe you just landed a fantastic engineering position. Or maybe you're heading into rehab because starting with honors math I flunked out of school and hit the skids. But it felt like I had to make a move, had to do what Vicky didn't want me to do. The totally wrong reason to go into an honors class, I know. Still, there it is.

It also hurts because I'm lonely. I've been thinking that maybe I don't know how to choose good friends, or that maybe the nature of friendship is that you have to put all your trust in this person who could at any second turn around and tear out your hair or rip your life to shreds. Friendship doesn't just allow that kind of trust, it practically requires it. That freaks me out a little, because of course the alternative is to have no friends at all, never trust or love anybody, which sounds pretty damn depressing.

Maybe it's just a mood, like I heard Mom explain to everybody after I made a scene at the Labor Day dinner party. I couldn't help it. Dr. Ferris asked if Vicky was there helping with me. I said no and offered him a sparkling cider. He took one and announced to all the guests that someday he might have to operate to stop me and Vicky from being joined at the hip. Ha-ha. Everybody giggled. Grown-ups, giggling. I thought I might cry, so I turned around, deposited the tray of sparkling ciders in the sink, and went up to my room. It doesn't feel like just a mood.

On the other hand, I'm feeling like maybe I'm stronger, or at least maybe more interesting, because of what happened. If the woman with the earrings hadn't had a wide-open chest wound, the fact that she was proud of her earrings would not have been at all remarkable. She'd have been just some woman who was more interested in material things—in chintzy jewelry, no less—than in major questions of life and death. Maybe what I found out by having my chest torn open and my heart yanked out is that I have a survival instinct. So what if I'm lousy at choosing friends—my last-second judgment is reliable, maybe.

I already wrote a letter to Nadine, who went to visit her parents before college started, thanking her again for letting me keep *Beloved*. If she doesn't write back, that's okay. I hope she and Henry stay together, or that if they don't work out, it will be at a time when Henry realizes I'm the perfect girl for him.

Maybe there will be some people in the high school who might be like me. Whatever that means. Nice reformed shoplifters opposed to smoking who can wiggle their pinkie toes. Who am I? I mean, what do I turn out to be like? I wish I could just peek ahead for five minutes and know that I turn out okay. I wouldn't even have to see the details, but it would be pretty reassuring to find out you're all right, Future Me.

I was taking off my brown turtleneck last night, the night before high school started, and I saw myself in the mirror with the hair all pulled off my face, caught in the turtleneck, and thought, with absolute clarity, This is what I'll look like when I'm thirty. I didn't hate it. That's something.

Oh, I should get this down: I've started eating again. I'm on a health-food kick and have been using the juicer Dad gave Mom for her birthday last year. Carrot juice is vile stuff, but I'm hoping to become radiant. That's what the book that came with the juicer said would happen if I drink it. Maybe I'll never be totally un-weird about food like I was when I was little, but I think I'll try to be in control of my life in other ways. I've proven that I am able to starve myself. Oh, there's a talent. Wow, impressive. Time to move on to other stuff.

Like singing. I tried out for chorale today. Turns out I'm an alto, and the chorale teacher was so happy, because they're short on altos with powerful voices. I stopped trying to lose my voice. Now I'm working on developing it. Something about me may as well be powerful.

I also might join the poetry magazine—there's a meeting tomorrow—and the track team. I think it would be really neat to get a high school letter, and although I'm still horribly slow, nobody gets cut from the track team. I like that kind of odds of making it. Being on a team could be a good experience, all of us coming together, stuff like that. In the movies, being on a team is always a real character-building thing. And maybe I'll meet some people who won't look at me like they wish I would hurry up and die already.

I think the thing with Vicky is going to hurt for a long time. Does it still hurt, Future Me?

She passed me at my locker today. I tried to blend into the metal. Will she really be able to make high school hell for me? Or maybe only ninth grade. If it's only ninth grade, I think I can survive it. ONE DAY AT A TIME, the bumper sticker on Dad's truck says.

Someday, mark Grace's words, Vicky will come and apologize to me. Maybe by then I'll be able to forgive her. Or maybe I'll publish this whole journal, and she'll see herself and apologize. Ha. That'll show her. I'll have to type it first, though, and so far I don't know how to type.

"You'll surprise them all," Grace said. "Mark my words. But not me. I expect great things from you." I took a walk with her down the beach during volleyball the day before she left the Island. We talked things out and forgave each other. She said, Isn't Jason a good kisser? Did he ever run his finger down the front of your neck? It was too weird a conversation, and I said I really had to get back to The Nail Place. I only wanted to straighten things out, end things nicely.

"You're so nice," Grace said.

I told her, "Yeah, but I'm working on it." She didn't get it. I say things just to amuse myself, sometimes. At least I keep myself entertained.

Maybe I'll call Keiko and ask her if she wants to borrow a really good book, and lend her my copy of *Beloved*. Or maybe not. Maybe by October, I'll find an enchanted spot and a friend to go there with, or maybe I'll just have zillions of questions on uncountable numbers of tracks in my head for the rest of my life.

Oh, well. What can I say? I survived. I'm surviving. Maybe at least I'm not quite so vanilla anymore. Stuff happened to me. It's mine.

So, Future Me, what do you think? Are you somebody I would like? Are you somebody who would like me? If yes, I wish you could come back in time and take the locker next to mine. It's a killer walking the halls alone.

Why do I feel like I have to sum things up? I still want a neat ending to this part of my life. So that's how my childhood ended, and I lived happily ever after. Fat chance. I have to read a chapter about Bushmen in the Kalahari Desert and then find the hypotenuses of fourteen triangles. I keep looking for ultimate answers, but maybe there aren't any or maybe I'm not looking in the right places, because in the section marked ANSWERS in the back of my geometry book, there's only a bunch of numbers, and all I can find to stare at in the refrigerator is five carrots and a jar of no-fat mayonnaise.

An excerpt from Rachel Vail's

KEVIN LAZARUS STOPPED in front of me in the
hall, turned around, and asked me if I was ready for the bio
quiz. While he was asking, he touched my hair. It was a
strand on the front left side. He twirled it around his index
finger and then let go. When he did that I couldn't remember if I was even taking bio this year. I think I may actually
have said "duh." Kevin smiled and strolled into class. I sat
down right there in the hall because my knees had lost their
ability to support me.

I should say right up front that I don't like Kevin
Lazarus. He French-kissed his last girlfriend twelve times
at one party, with everybody watching (and counting),

and broke up with her the next day online. He is exactly the kind of boy who has never interested me at all. But there I was on the floor outside bio.

"What are you doing on the floor?" my best friend, Tess, asked me.

"Waiting for you," I lied.

I got up and followed her into class. I should also say that at that point I had never kissed anybody. No interest, for one, and also I had some romantic ideas about how my first kiss would happen. Maybe there would be a tree above us, maybe some music would be playing. Tess thinks atmosphere is a cliché and I should just get the first kiss over with already. Since before ninth grade started, she has been trying to convince me to kiss George Jacobson.

George Jacobson is a really nice guy. One time last May during a debate in social studies, George said that, though he disagreed with my premise, it was clear that I was an independent thinker and a moral person. It was a slightly weird moment. After class, Tess said wow, George Jacobson is totally in love with you. I said no, he's just a nice guy, a gentleman. All the mothers like George. Everybody does. I like George. Good old George.

Kissing George would be like kissing my cousin.

But as I sat down at my desk in bio I realized that I

was ready to kiss someone. I was suddenly, overwhelm-ingly, sick of waiting. I couldn't remember what exactly I'd been waiting for anymore. Tess has fallen in love with all three boys she's kissed, and she said there was no way I could possibly understand how awesome and overpower-ing that kind of love is without experiencing it for myself. She said it was beyond describing. Every single experience in my entire life has been describable. In fact, I have described most of them to Tess.

Kevin may be a jerk but he had scrunched his eyes when he looked at me.

Tess passed me a note: "You okay?"

I realized I hadn't started my bio quiz, hadn't even turned it over. I flipped the paper and filled in the answers. *Yes, Kevin, I did study.* I flipped it back over and picked up Tess's note again. She is my best friend. We tell each other everything. She would be happy if I finally got a crush on somebody, maybe especially Kevin Lazarus, given my rants against him. Tess is a big fan of irony.

I didn't write back, pretending instead I was still work-ing on the bio quiz. It might be a passing weakness, I decided, like a tickle in your nose that never grows into a sneeze. I would probably stop thinking about kissing Kevin by the end of the period, I hoped, anyway, and return to my rational, self-controlled self.

Well, a week later I was almost fully back to normal. My proof is that as I was following Kevin off the bus at school the next Tuesday morning, I was deep in thought not about what would it be like to kiss him or how cute it is that the bottom bit of his hair curls up where it hits his collar, but about which is better, peanut butter with M&Ms or peanut butter with chocolate chips. At that exact moment, Kevin stopped in front of me again.

"Hey," he said.

I almost swallowed my gum.

"You walk home."

This was true. It was a statement of fact. It felt like an accusation. I started to shake my head.

"I thought you did."

Caught. What could I say? *The cover-up is worse than the crime* is what flashed through my head. "Um," I said. "Not until, um, after school."

He looked a little baffled at that, reasonably.

That broke my nervousness; I snorted a laugh. "Oh, really?" I couldn't help mocking myself. I put on a space-cadet voice and asked myself, "You mean you don't walk home immediately after getting off the bus in the morning?"

He grinned at me. "Come 'ere," he said, and grabbed my hand. The warning bell had rung. It was time to get in to school. I'm never late for school.

His hand was warm, and it was in mine.

As discreetly as possible I pressed my right fist against my mouth and stuck my gum to the back of it, just in case this was going to turn into a kissing-type thing. Even in my in experience, I knew you are not supposed to have gum in your mouth while you kiss.

Kevin led me quickly around the side of the building, then stopped. I managed not to crash into him. I tried to look calm, cool, unperturbed. I told myself not to laugh, especially not a snorting kind of laugh. "Wha—what did—"

And then he kissed me.

There I was, pressed up against the brick wall, kissing Kevin. A decorative sticking-out brick was digging into my backbone, but I didn't want to wreck my first kiss by readjusting. I squeezed my eyes shut and tried to concentrate.

I wanted to be mature and focus on the kiss, but even beyond the stabbing pain in my back and the fact that the late bell had long since rung by then, I was really distracted by wondering what kind of sick French person invented this bizarre way of kissing. I'm not even supposed to share a bottle of water with anyone because of germs.

When we finished kissing I had to wipe my mouth dry. We didn't say good-bye or anything. I took my gum off the back of my hand and put it in my mouth. Luckily there was still some mint flavor left because the taste in my mouth was a little mildewy. I thought, maybe this is what Kevin's mouth always tastes like—Ew. To keep myself from gagging, I tried to concentrate on the mintiness and also on the fact that it was the kind of gum that supposedly kills the germs that cause bad breath so, well, maybe it could kill whatever germs Kevin might've given me. Which made me that much more queasy.

We started walking toward the entrance of school. I let my hand dangle in case he wanted to hold it again but apparently he didn't.

I picked up the pace as we got to the door and, crossing the lobby, scanned the halls for Tess. She wasn't there. Surprisingly I felt a little relieved. I wanted to not tell her all about it for a few minutes. I wasn't sure yet whether it had been a describable or indescribable experience. My first kiss. Well, it was disgusting, but I liked it. Uh-oh. Describable?

I heard Kevin's footsteps behind me, coming closer. Maybe the experience was still going on, and that's why I wasn't sure. We were approaching the corner near the office and Kevin was catching up to me. I slowed down. Should I spit out my gum again, in case he was coming back for more?

An excerpt from Rachel Vail's

do-over

I DON'T GET girls. I don't mean get like *get*, which is also true, but I mean I really don't get what's up with them. Why can't they just be normal?

Like at the Halloween party. We were playing Spin the Bottle, and this girl Sheila spun me. I guess I kissed her okay because later on she picked me for Seven in Heaven.

I'd never actually played Seven in Heaven before, so I wasn't positive how you go about it. I mean, obviously you're supposed to make out with each other. I knew that much. I just wasn't sure how you get started. You're in a dark closet alone with some seventh-grade girl you barely

1

know but you've already kissed once. It's different, though. Out there it's light and everybody's around.

"Hi," I said, to break the ice. "It's dark in here." She was leaning against the side wall of the closet with her arms behind her. Waiting for me to do something? I didn't want her to think I'd never played before. She was dressed up like a bum, but I could see by the light coming in under the closet door that she looked pretty anyway. Long hair really does it to me. "You're sexy," I started to say, but in the middle it got messed up and came out as "Your socks."

"My socks?"

"They're nice," I said, and leaned against the closet door. I was sweating. Good thing I started using deodorant.

"They are?" I couldn't even see her socks.

"Yeah," I said, and my voice squeaked. I lowered it and cleared my throat. "You have seductive socks." Doug says it's important for a guy to have a good rap. It makes girls like you.

Sheila slid down onto the floor and started to cry, holding her face in her hands. This is what I mean about girls not being normal. I watched her for a second and then felt embarrassed, so I counted the suits hanging on a rod over Sheila's head. They looked like thirteen ghosts of businessmen, all watching me screw up.

2

"What?"

"Forget it," she said, through her hands. I turned around and banged my head against the door. You try to be nice to them and you make them cry.

She snorted and started breathing heavy. Everybody outside must've thought I was really getting somewhere with this girl. I sat down on the floor against the door.

"Don't breathe so loud."

"Sorr-ee," she said.

"No," I whispered, "I don't want it to sound like, you know . . . right in front of everybody. . . ."

"Do I kiss okay?" She lifted her head up and wiped her nose with the side of her hand.

"Yeah," I said. "You kiss really nice." I tried to shift over nearer to her, since if she was talking about kissing, maybe she was giving me a hint. I got up on my knees so I could move closer, but there was a turtle-neck wrapped around my right leg. I pulled it off and crawled toward her.

"I wish . . ." she said, and breathed in fast, which sounded, if anybody was listening, like we were really doing it.

"What?" I whispered, trying to encourage her to keep it down. I was so close I could smell her. She smelled clean.

"It's just . . . forget it. You kiss okay, too," she said, and

3

stood up. I was still on my knees.

"I do?"

She sponged off her face with her sleeve and nodded.

"Thanks." I stood up and tried to think of something to say to her, but I have no rap at all. Instead I folded the turtleneck and put it on top of a pile of old clothes.

Sheila stared at the door until some geek with a striped sheet over his head opened it and made a stupid comment. You'd never know she'd been crying. She went running up to a bunch of girls and started whispering and giggling. I watched her and wondered if she meant it, about the kissing, or if she was just being polite.

My turn to choose, and since every guy in the room wanted her, I chose Amy. She closed the closet door, behind her. She's not even that pretty to me. It's just she was The One, if you know what I mean.

"What's your name again?"

"Whitman Levy," I said.

"You on the soccer team?" Lots of guys from the team showed up dressed as soccer players, same as me. My mother thought I should go as Mozart, so she bought me a white wig and said I could carry her old violin. Right. She always came up with costumes I had to explain at people's doors.

"Yeah," I said. "I'm a forward. Left wing."

"You wanna make out?"

"Yeah," I said. "Do you?"

"I guess," she said. I had backed up by this time against the thirteen suits. Nobody budged. Nothing happened. Right, I thought, my move. I pushed off against the wall and went right up to her and put my lips against hers and my hands against the door behind her head. I felt her boobs against me and thought, Holy. Every guy here wishes he were me right now. Only problem was, I was still thinking of Sheila and imagining it was her I was pressed up against.

Amy pushed me away. "You're gonna break my jaw," she said, and started rubbing her face. I sat down and waited on the pile of clothes for the geek to let us out. I guess I'm really not that great a kisser.

I went back to Spin the Bottle and hoped I would get another chance to try with Sheila, or at least maybe talk to her. She had this way of raising her eyebrows when she looked at you. Out in the light she smiled a lot, and her socks really were sort of seductive. Argyles. Green ones. Maybe I should ask her out, I thought, even if she is a grade below me.

Before I got up my guts, though, we were kicked out by the mother of the girl whose party it was because we didn't know how to behave. "I was *being* hayve," Mackey said, even though he was the one who started the food fight in the first place. Doug and I were sleeping over at Mackey's. It was within walking distance, so no mothers would have to pick us up and also so on the way we could Silly String some cars.

Sheila smiled at me while I was shaking my can of Silly String by the curb with the guys. When I went up to say good-bye, though, she ran over to this girl Andi, who was dressed exactly like her, and they started whispering. Andi is black and has short hair, and Sheila's white with long, but their costumes were the same—Andi had on argyle socks, too, and baggy jeans and a plaid shirt, same as Sheila. Every time I looked at Andi all night, she was staring at Doug. I don't think Doug noticed.

Sheila and Andi held on to each other's sleeves and whispered, looking at me, Doug, and Mackey over their shoulders. We Silly Stringed their shoes. They acted all pissed and bent down to clean them off like we had ruined something valuable, when it was just old beat-up sneakers, and anyway Silly String is completely harmless.

I think maybe girls are a different species. Life would be so much easier if I could stop thinking about them all the time.